ESPRIT DE CORPS

ESPRIT DE CORPS
(The Spirit of the Corps)

A Novel
Inspired by
Actual Events

Herbert H. Roebuck
with
Connie Bertelsen Young

SUNSTONE
PRESS

SANTA FE

Sunstone books may be purchased for educational, business, or sales promotional use. For information please write: Special Markets Department, Sunstone Press, P.O. Box 2321, Santa Fe, New Mexico 87504-2321.

Book and cover design › Vicki Ahl
Body typeface › Cambria
Printed on acid-free paper
∞
eBook 978-1-61139-435-1

Library of Congress Cataloging-in-Publication Data

Names: Roebuck, Herbert H., 1928- | Young, Connie Bertelsen, 1947-
Title: Esprit de corps = The spirit of the corps : a novel inspired by actual
   events / by Herbert H. Roebuck with Connie Bertelsen Young.
Other titles: Spirit of the corps
Description: Santa Fe : Sunstone Press, 2016.
Identifiers: LCCN 2015036215 | ISBN 9781632930941 (softcover : alk. paper)
Subjects: LCSH: Vietnam War, 1961-1975--Fiction. | United States. Marine
   Corps--Fiction. | GSAFD: War stories.
Classification: LCC PS3618.O365 E86 2016 | DDC 813/.6--dc23
LC record available at http://lccn.loc.gov/2015036215

Sunstone Press is committed to minimizing our environmental impact on the planet. The paper used in this book is from responsibly managed forests. Our printer has received Chain of Custody (CoC) certification from: The Forest Stewardship Council™ (FSC®), Programme for the Endorsement of Forest Certification™ (PEFC™), and The Sustainable Forestry Initiative® (SFI®).

The FSC® Council is a non-profit organization, promoting the environmentally appropriate, socially beneficial and economically viable management of the world's forests. FSC® certification is recognized internationally as a rigorous environmental and social standard for responsible forest management.

WWW.SUNSTONEPRESS.COM
SUNSTONE PRESS / POST OFFICE BOX 2321 / SANTA FE, NM 87504-2321 /USA
(505) 988-4418 / ORDERS ONLY (800) 243-5644 / FAX (505) 988-1025

Dedication

This book is dedicated
to the memory of all who
died or were disabled from
Agent Orange in Vietnam.

Blessed be the LORD my Rock,
Who trains my hands for war,
And my fingers for battle.
                    —Psalm 144:1 NKJV

Contents

Introduction

I was inspired to write this stimulating adventure of life and emotions after listening to the hilarious yarns which Herbert Roebuck, former Master Sergeant in the Marine Corps, asked me to write. In many ways, this book is a reflection of his personal life experience.

The story begins during the War in Vietnam and highlights the colorful life of Will Brown, a small town boy from West Virginia who wants to change his life. Will is an inexperienced youth who gets cold feet when he's with his childhood sweetheart, cringes at confrontations and is intimidated by loud mouth bullies. He dreams of becoming a Marine so he can become the man he longs to be. Sidesplitting antics of this main character and his buddies include their experiences in a rowdy Southern bar, training of an uncooperative dog, embarrassing encounters, a traumatic night at the dance, a wedding, recruitment, survival techniques and numerous endeavors as Will is ultimately molded into a Marine.

Will's faith, family and friends are an integral part of this book. And along with bringing laughter, it will remind one of the horrifying price that is, and was, paid for war. While in the trenches of enemy territory, Will's life is changed as he sees for the first time the bloody insides of a human being who has been blown up, as he watches brave men give there lives to rescue others, and as he endures hardships far away from home.

Although a fictional tale, within these pages readers will find details about the Marine Corps' strenuous and excellent training at Parris Island, Camp Lejeune and Camp Pendleton during the sixties, and the Marine's incredible fortitude throughout the war in Vietnam.

There are few entities on earth that compare to the United States Marine Corps with their reputation of discipline, perseverance and endurance. One could say their notability is a supernatural fact, mainly because this institution was surely blessed by Almighty God to protect and defend America. This is a fresh, stimulating and believable adventure, embracing the seasons of life, hope, hate and love.

There is a time for everything, and a season for every activity under the heavens: a time to be born and a time to die, a time to plant and a time to uproot, a time to kill and a time to heal, a time to tear down and a time to build, a time to weep and a time to laugh, a time to mourn and a time to dance, a time to scatter stones and a time to gather them, a time to embrace and a time to refrain from embracing, a time to search and a time to give up, a time to keep and a time to throw away, a time to tear and a time to mend, a time to be silent and a time to speak, a time to love and a time to hate, a time for war and a time for peace. (Ecclesiastes 3:1-8 NIV)

—Connie Bertelsen Young

1

West Virginia Farm 1965

A young, bright-eyed raccoon paced back and forth near the chicken coop which appeared to lean precariously, although actually secure enough, on one side of the barn at the Brown's sharecropper farm. The moon shining on the animal's fur made the fur appear the same color as the siding on the barn which had aged over the years in West Virginia weather. The exploring coon had already attempted to get inside the smokehouse on the other side of the barn, but it was locked up tight the night before after the owner hung a new carcass on a huge rusty hook. But now, the chicken eggs beckoned the animal from a straw nest shelf.

In attempt to get nearer the anticipated feast, the coon managed to climb on top of a nearby sugar cane grinder, which might be hitched to a mule when the sun was up, but chicken wire, covering a portion of the cages, forbade his entry to the pen that way.

Twenty-year-old, Will Brown, sprawled upon his comfortable feather mattress, suddenly opened his eyes as he was awakened by raucous chicken chatter and automatically jumped out of bed. Dressed in long underwear with the tailgate unbuttoned, exposing his bare rear, he hurriedly grabbed his double-barrel shotgun, cocking both barrels as he exited the house.

Will grimaced as his bare feet were greased with chicken leavings between his toes, and warily moved toward the coop. By this time, the disturbance has awakened Radar, and the aging farm hound, customarily late and disinterested in responding to intruders nowadays, lazily sneaked up behind Will. As Will bent down, letting the folding door to the chicken coop rest on his back to look inside, Radar stuck his cold nose to Will's bare rear causing him to fire both barrels, killing three Rhode Island Reds.

The raccoon was long gone, disappearing in the cotton field when Will's crotchety dad, Walter Brown, carrying his own shotgun, also in long underwear and barefooted, slammed the back screen door of the house and approached the barnyard yelling, "What in the hell is going on?"

Hesitating to go beyond the back porch, Will's mother, Velma Brown eventually appeared in her nightgown and nightcap, followed by her other son, thirteen-year-old Milford, both with startled looks on their faces. Her daughter, six-year old, Becky, a little blond girl with disheveled hair, wearing a pink-flowered, flannel nightgown, faded from many washes, peeked out a window, stretching and yawning, undaunted by the noise.

Morning sun rays began to bring light on Will as he washed the sticky covering off his feet with a bucket of water drawn from the well. Then, despite his reluctance to explain what caused the commotion to a waiting audience, whose perturbed faces indicated they were not appreciating this early morning escapade, he described the embarrassing scenario.

Eventually Milford crawled into the chicken coop to collect some of what would surely be the main course for dinner. He handed the bloody chickens to his brother and Velma handed him the now empty water bucket to collect eggs while he was at it.

As father and sons went back to the house for breakfast, Walter pointed upward, studied the sky and advised, "It's going to rain!"

Will shook his head, "That's jet vapor you're lookin' at, Dad. Them aren't clouds."

But Walter insisted, "Mark my words, son. It's gonna rain."

While Velma prepared food in cast iron pans in the comparatively old-fashioned kitchen for 1965, little Becky set the table for breakfast—as she did since she was three.

After the five Browns enjoyed a hearty meal of fresh eggs, smoked bacon and biscuits and gravy, Velma grabbed the old drip style coffee pot and refilled her husband and Will's cups with the steaming liquid. They heard a lazy woof from Radar as a boy was hastily riding a wobbly red Schwinn up the driveway. Velma stopped what she was doing and listened attentively until a thud was heard against the front door. The newspaper landed successfully for a change, and her newly planted Chrysanthemums were preserved, at least until the next delivery.

By seven o'clock, Milford and little Becky were out the door and waited for the school bus at the end of the driveway where it met a partially paved road. Will remained at the cleared breakfast table with another cup of coffee and studied the Want Ads in the newspaper.

Walter, dressed in a faded green and grey checked flannel shirt and light blue overalls with patched holes in the knees, had been working since six o'clock. Slamming the back door as usual, and getting a frown for slamming it from Velma, he entered the room and glared at Will. Will, oblivious to his glare, pointed at the Want Ad he was reading and asked, "What's a rezoom?"

Velma chuckled. "That's not rezoom. It's resume. They want you to write down what workin' experience you got."

Walter listened to Velma's explanation and moved behind Will. With a sarcastic grin on his face he thumped his finger on Will's back and said, "You need to get up off your lazy ass and put your boots on and I'll give you some workin' experience!"

Will scratched his head, folded up the newspaper, gulped the last of the coffee and proceeded to get ready for a day of work on the farm.

That afternoon, Will was working in the field when he saw Milford and little Becky getting off the bus. Milford made a beeline for Will as soon as he saw him.

Seeing the downcast expression on Milford's face, Will asked, "What's the matter with you?"

Looking at his feet, Milford spluttered, "Frankie Ragsdale and one of his friends jumped out of his car when I got off the bus in front of the school this morning...and they stole my lunch!"

Will put his hand on his little brother's shoulder and comforted, "Don't worry Milford, we'll get 'em. Come on." He led him to the barn and they went inside where, among other items found on a farm, there were several old wagon wheels, barrels, three crooked sawhorses with saddles, antique collections of tools, ropes and a pitchfork leaning on a couple hay bales. At the very back of the barn, Will had several animals in small cages, some of which he had nursed back to health after finding them wounded. Among the animals was a ferocious wolverine.

Will produced a dusty old suitcase from a spider-webbed corner, and after a few attempts using a pole and lasso, Will skillfully managed the wolverine and placed him in the suitcase. After the bouncing of the suitcase subsided a bit, he directed Milford. "Frankie and his friends will be coming back from the Four Corners store and up the road as usual any minute. Quick! Run out and set the suitcase on the road and we'll see what happens."

Milford smiled broadly and took off running with the suitcase. Then he and his brother hid and waited for the returning car. Minutes later, Frankie's car could be seen coming up the road and then slowing down. They heard loud music blaring from the car radio. The car stopped and the passengers curiously peered out the windows. Then one of Frankie's friends quickly jumped out of the car, and after looking around, picked up the suitcase and returned to the car with it. They drove off, burning rubber.

The car went a short distance when suddenly all four doors blew open and the occupants scattered. Will and Milford gave each other a high five and walked to the house laughing hysterically.

When the two got to the door, Radar followed them in. With flour on the tip of her nose, an apron tied around her waist and her hands on her hips, Velma demanded, "Get that critter outta here! Until you housebreak that mutt, I ain't havin' him in my house!"

As the sun was setting and Velma placed her perfectly prepared, crispy fried chicken on a platter, it began to rain. Smirking, Walter came in from a day of work, slammed the screen door and said, "I told you so."

When Little Becky had set the table, the members of the Brown family were washed up and seated for dinner (along with one lazy hound hidden under the table, patiently waiting for secret offerings).

Everyone bowed their heads while little Becky parroted the customary table prayer. "Come Lord Jesus, be our guest. And let this food to us be blessed! Amen."

The raindrops began to vigorously pelt the roof as the contented family enjoyed the mouth-watering fried chicken, mashed potatoes, homemade rolls, churned butter, and garden fresh turnips, followed by berry pudding with sweet cream for dessert.

2

First Love

In the morning, Will gave Milford and little Becky a ride to school in his 1936 Ford pickup, dropping them off and waiting for them to go inside the fenced area while he kept an eye out for Frankie Ragsdale. After waving goodbye, Will drove to the Beckley Sav-A-Lot market where his close friend, Pete Springer worked as a stock person.

Will found his friend in the break room and noticed the room had a distinctive odor. Twenty-year-old, long-legged Pete sat backward on a chair and was eating with his fingers from a can of sardines. He offered two fingers full of his silvery breakfast to Will when he entered. Will gave him a scowl and pulled up a wood crate to sit on. Smirking and knowing Will hated sardines, Pete continued stuffing them in his mouth, licking his lips and rolling his eyes. Then he spoke.

"I heard they're havin' a dance at the Legion Hall Saturday night." He stood up and grabbed a soda cracker from the box left on the break room card table and continued, carefully watching his friend for a response. "Why don't you ask Laverne to go? I'll ask Linda and we can all go together."

Will looked at the ceiling and studied the light bulb hanging from the center. He shook his head. "I don't know. She belongs to that Holy Roller Church and I don't think they like dancin'. Besides, I can't dance anyways."

"Well, I noticed they did plenty dancin' in the church aisles at that revival."

"Yeah, but that's different."

Unable to produce enthusiasm in his friend, Pete took the empty sardine can and crushed it with his large calloused hands. "Ah Will, what you have is an incurable inferiority complex. My brother, you need help!"

Pete pranced around the break room using the body language with his arms and hands like a great orator. "You're too shy and have no courage. You've sat by Laverne when all of us go to the movies on Saturday nights since the eighth grade. Broaden your romantic horizons and give the poor girl a break. Do something different. I've never even seen you kiss her."

Will had a defensive look in his eyes when he responded, "I kissed her plenty times...but that's none of your business!"

Pete appeared amazed. "Yeah? But did you ever give her flowers or gifts? Nope. I know you. Your love life ain't movin'. You need to get counseling, talk to a preacher...or maybe you should just join the Marines. Maybe they can help your wimpy ass."

Will had a strange look on his face as he processed Pete's enthusiastic advice. He had to admit he was more inspired about joining the Marines than going to a dumb dance, but he knew he'd better do something, because deep down, he loved Laverne.

Pete kept pressing, "Ask her to the dance, Will!"

Suddenly, the door to the break room opened and the heavy-set Sav-A-Lot manager appeared, not a happy camper. The red-faced manager pointed at the clock, but before he said a word, he stopped and sniffed the air. Then he picked up the smelly, crumpled sardine can, shook his head, sighed and at a loss for words, cursed silently at the floor. This wasn't the first time Pete took too much break time.

Quickly removing himself from the hostile environment of the Sav-A-Lot Market break room, Will got in his truck and headed down the highway towards Laverne's work place. On the side of the road he saw a United States Marine Corps recruiting billboard showing handsome Marines dressed in blues with the caption:

THE MARINE CORPS BUILDS MEN BODY, SOUL AND SPIRIT.

Sighing, he wondered what he would look like in one of those Marine uniforms. When he pulled up to the Raleigh County Recorder's office where Laverne worked, Will was just in time to see Laverne coming down the side-walk on her way to work. Waving at her, he parked his truck in the Recorder's parking lot, rolled down his window, whistled at her and watched her move towards him, smiling.

Laverne Alderman, a slender, nineteen-year-old, brunette beauty, was raised by her single mother because her dad, Jess Alderman, left when she was only four. Her feminine carriage belied her ability to be tough when necessary, but her mother had taught her the survival attitudes that she herself had, and she didn't back down to anyone. Laverne had the reputation of busting bullies in the head with her books while she was in grammar school, and nowadays, the men at the Recorder's office knew better than to cross the line. Nevertheless, a steadfast faith and love for God was clearly observed in her actions and it made Will stand in awe of what to him was a mysterious personality. Through her he learned, true Christians weren't weak people who needed a crutch like some people thought.

Will didn't know it, but when Laverne was ten, she announced to her mother that she was most certainly going to marry Will. Her mind never changed and her heart was sealed. Despite his shyness around other people, Laverne saw a strength and integrity in Will that she knew God would develop into the confident man she wanted for a husband. Although he was not the handsomest guy who showed interest in her, she liked him best. He kept her laughing at his antics, and right then she couldn't help herself for smiling at him for whistling at her.

With Laverne's pretty face beaming at him and the dimples in her cheeks appearing, Will suddenly felt weak. Yeah, maybe he did need counseling like Pete had suggested a little while ago.

Laverne opened the passenger door of Will's truck and jumped in and sat down beside him. "What are you doin' here?"

Feeling a little dumbfounded at first, Will stumbled for words until they finally spilled out. "I...I...was wonderin'...if you'd like to do something different on Saturday night?"

Laverne was curious. "Like what?"

Will continued, "There's a dance at the Legion Hall."

Eyes big, Laverne asked, "Can you dance?"

Will explained, "Naw...but Pete told me about the dance. He wants to take Linda, and He wants me to take you."

Laverne pretended to get a cross look on her face. "Hmmm. PETE wants you to take me." She paused thinking it over, tilted her head, fluttered her long eyelashes and then looked seriously into his eyes questioning, "Will Brown, do YOU want to take me?"

Will self-consciously put his tongue in his cheek and rolled it around. "Well, I wouldn't ask you if I didn't."

Although a little disappointed in his response to her question, after a moment or two Laverne acceded to the invitation, betraying her cross facade and revealing her delight. "Okay. Let's go. At least we can sit there and enjoy the music!"

Satisfied that it was settled, they both got out of the truck and Will walked with Laverne inside the Recorder's office building, parting with her at the time clock. He hung out for a minute because he wanted to see his friend, Charlie, who was on security duty.

Charlie Shipman was 6'3" tall and built like a brick house. Although underneath his intimidating muscular physique there was a tender personality as soft as mush, he earned the respect of the locals for his strength and ability to take control of difficult individuals. There was a tattoo of a heart on his right arm with the word, "Mom."

Charlie stuffed a plug of chewing tobacco inside his cheek and walked back outside with Will. Charlie loved to talk, and working at the County Recorder's Office, he heard a lot of gossip and liked to share new information with his buddies.

"Hey Will...did you hear about Frankie Ragsdale?"

With all the control he could muster, Will quickly put a blank expression on his face and attentively waited for the spiel. Charlie laughed uncontrollably at himself as he related the funny suitcase story. Then he shared more of the silly local chinwag, always embellishing the stories, until Will was in stitches too.

Before he got back in his truck, Will finally had the opportunity to ask his inimitable source of information a question. "How do you housebreak a dog?"

After thoughtfully shooting a brown stream of tobacco from his mouth, Charlie advised,

"Well...it ain't pretty. But first, you rub his nose in his own crap. Then you roll up a newspaper and beat him with it. Then, throw him out the window."

On the way back home, Will spotted the enticing Marine billboard again. Pulling off on a side road he parked at an angle to look back at it. The truth was, he had always wanted to be a Marine. The idea of enlisting had been pulling at the back of his mind since high school. Somehow after Pete's corny lecture, he couldn't quit thinking about it. Since he graduated, nearly two years had already passed while he worked full time with his dad at the farm. But what would his dad say if he left the farm?

3

Once Upon an Outhouse

Late that afternoon at home, Will found Milford sitting cross-legged on the porch, cleaning his bolt action 410 shotgun. He watched Milford place a shell in the chamber to check extraction, but when he slid the bolt forward, he accidentally fired the gun. The fired round hit one end of the hammock which was drawn between two trees. Radar was sleeping on the swing, and with the force of the swing's disconnection, it catapulted the yelping Radar airborne into the yard, making his long ears look like wings.

Shocked by the firing, Will shouted at his brother, "What did you do?"

Milford wailed shakily, "I never touched the trigger. I slid the bolt forward and it just went off!"

Will corrected him. "Milford, no weapon will fire unless you pull the trigger."

Embarrassed by his mistake, Milford tossed the shotgun and a shell to Will. "Okay, smart ass, you try it."

Will carefully placed the shell in the chamber, but when he slid the bolt forward, he blew a hole in the outhouse door, adding a full moon to the half-moon already there.

Walter, came out from the barn with a frown on his face and demanded, "What in tarnation has been goin' on out here?" Radar, who had hid for cover after the first incident, crept behind him with his tail between his legs.

Milford scowled at his brother and responded sarcastically, "Will was just tryin' to shoot the moon."

That evening, while Will was patching up the outhouse door, his older brother, twenty-two year old Jimmy T drove up in a shiny new car. Jimmy T was the owner of a dry cleaning business in Charleston.

Jimmy T walked up to Will keenly observing the damage. "I see you've been havin' a little target practice, brother."

Will turned around and laid his tools down to greet his brother, happy to see him. "Well, somethun like that."

Jimmy T suggested, "You know, I've been wanting to pay a contractor to install twentieth century bathroom plumbing in the house as a gift to mom. Maybe you could convince dad to let me do that?"

Will studied his brother and kicked at the loose dirt on the ground. "Why don't you go ask him?"

Jimmy T looked down at his shiny black shoes that were getting dusty and admitted, "I'd like to see Mom, but if I go inside, Dad and I will get in a big argument and upset her. I don't think he'll ever forgive me for leaving the farm."

It was the very thing that kept Will from his dream of joining the Marines, but he tried to encourage Jimmy T, hoping his next statement was true.

"Time has a way of healin' most things."

The sun had gone all the way down when the two brothers hugged and Jimmy T drove away with his headlights on. Velma spotted the car lights and came out of the house. "How long has Jimmy T been here?"

Will put his arm around his mother and said, "He was in a hurry but he said he'd stop by later this week and give you a hug."

When they went inside the house, they found Walter brooding. "Well, what did your rich brother want?"

Will used the opportunity to explain what his brother had offered to do, but Walter's gloomy face immediately made it clear that he didn't appreciate the offer. "Lord have mercy. I've been crappin' in my yard for over thirty years, and I'm sure as hell not gonna start crappin' in my house! Next time you see him, tell him no thanks."

Disgruntled and moody, Walter started to sit down in his favorite chair, but thinking of something else, he stood up, and shook his finger at Will and stormed, "And while we're on the subject of crappin' in the house...You need to train Radar to quit crappin' in the house!"

Will promised, "I'm workin' on it."

4

Dance at the Legion Hall

Dressed in her newly sewn, blue flowered dress with a ruffled full skirt, black baby doll shoes and her mother's tiny sapphire necklace, Laverne placed a dab of her Evening in Paris perfume on her wrist. Then after presenting herself to her mother who showed her approval, she began pacing back and forth in front of the living room window, anticipating Will's arrival.

Nina Alderman sat with a knitting project in her lap and watched her daughter. Finally, she asked, "Why are you so nervous? He's an easy-going boy and a nice, ordinary sharecropper's son."

Laverne rolled her eyes at the ceiling and kept pacing. Her mother continued. "Did you know Hollis Ragsdale owns the Brown farm? I've always wondered why you aren't interested in dating Frankie Ragsdale."

Laverne stopped pacing and responded with annoyance. "Oh mother... This is the first time Will has asked me out on a real date. Only thing else we've done together is church and the movies with our friends. And Frankie Ragsdale is a spoiled, vulgar, self-serving, loud-mouthed..." While she was still spilling out words of disapproval, she saw Will's pickup coming down the drive and her demeanor and her voice instantly changed. "He's here."

After Will rang the doorbell, Laverne escorted him into the house and asked him, "Where's Linda and Pete?"

Will pulled at the collar corner of his starched white shirt and handed Laverne a white carnation corsage, pricking his hand with the long, pearled straight pin which was attached to the stem. "Ouch."

He put his shaking hand to his mouth and licked the tiny wound and explained, "Linda wouldn't go with Pete. After she found out he lost his job, she lost interest." Will suddenly looked worried. "It's okay that you go with me anyhow, isn't it?"

Laverne's mother appeared in the entry way and greeted Will, commenting on the lovely corsage he brought for her daughter, taking it from her and pinning it on Laverne's dress.

Laverne, biting her lip with excitement looked pleadingly into her mother's eyes. "Mom...Linda and Pete weren't able to go tonight, so I'm going alone with Will."

Nina smiled and kissed Laverne on the cheek. "You kids go and have a good time. But don't stay out too late." Then standing at the front door, she waved at them as they drove away and out of sight. Remembering the look in her daughter's eyes when Laverne looked at Will, she spoke a prayer.

"What's going on here? Should I be worried?" A minute later, if anyone had been watching, they would have thought she received an audible response from God as she nodded, "Yes, I know you know what's best."

Many ages were represented at the dance at the Legion Hall and the large party room was filled with happy people, including one couple who were especially enjoying their time together. Laverne had helped Will loosen up by her reassurances, and although neither were used to dancing, they enjoyed holding hands and swinging to the music with the rest of the crowd. The general noise of socializing, laughing, and shoes slapping the floor to the music was almost as loud as the country western band.

After they were both out of breath from being involved in an energetic square dance, Will seated Laverne at a table near the back wall and offered to go and get some punch.

On the way back from the errand, Will passed a table where Frankie Ragsdale and his cohorts were seated. As Will passed, Frankie stuck out his foot and tripped him. Will fell to the floor with a clatter, taking an empty chair with him. The two cups full of red punch he carried were emptied and splattered on his white shirt. The music and the dancing stopped and everyone stared at Will, who was the laughingstock, especially at Frankie's table. Mortified, Will tried to get up and steady himself on the now slippery floor, but slipped and fell again. Uproarious shrieks of laughter from the callous onlookers increased without regard to Will's painful calamity.

Frankie loudly taunted him. "Hey farm boy, you need to clean up. Let's help him, boys!"

Frankie's friends physically took him out into the parking lot and squirted him with cold water from a hose. Then they held him up so Frankie could punch him. Meanwhile, as Frankie was pounding him, Laverne came outside and saw the ruffians pulling off Will's pants. Laverne furiously kicked and punched Frankie with all her strength. Frankie turned around to slap her, but Charlie Shipman, who was the designated security guard for the evening, had finally showed up. He grabbed Frankie's hand in midair, lifted him over his head, and threw him into the garbage bin. The crowd that had gathered was entertained by the spectacle and hooted and cheered.

After a moment, Frankie crawled out of the garbage bin with a bloody nose and flipped off Charlie. But when Charlie moved toward him, Frankie turned away and walked off with his friends, who had already moved to a precautionary distance from the notorious security guard.

The crowd had dispersed and music resumed inside the Legion Hall. Laverne and Will were left alone outside in the light of a bright full moon. Shivering and pulling up his pants, Will stood up, hanging his head in humiliation. With a tear running down her face, Laverne grabbed his hand and said, "C'mon, let's go home."

5

Decisions

Early Sunday morning, Will got in his pickup and drove straight over to the Marine recruiting billboard. He pulled off the highway and sat looking at it. The disgrace he experienced the night before made him know more than ever that he needed to change. Pete was right. He was "too shy and didn't have enough courage." He didn't even know how to defend himself. But there was the answer, printed clearly on the billboard.

THE MARINE CORPS BUILDS MEN BODY, SOUL AND SPIRIT.

For a few minutes he sat there and stared into space. Then he, grabbed the steering wheel, flexed his muscles, peeled out to get on the highway and yelled out the window as loud as he could to a puzzled truck driver with a Florida license plate, "I'm...gonna...be...a...Marine!"

About the same time that morning as Will pulled away from the billboard, Laverne had just finished praying hard for Will and their future while she kneeled at the altar of her church. She had also asked God to forgive her for the hatred she felt towards Frankie. She knew she shouldn't be judgmental, no matter how wicked she thought Frankie was. When the church service was over, she decided to go to Will's house and talk to him about their future.

Walter was surprised to see a pretty girl standing at his front door asking for Will. After she introduced herself, he invited her inside and they sat down at the kitchen table. Velma, Milford and little Becky hadn't returned from church yet, but the house already smelled of a roast which Velma had put in the oven before she left.

Walter poured a cup of coffee for himself and Laverne and asked, "What the heck happened at the dance last night? Will was a mess when he come home."

Laverne explained Will's regretful experience to Walter and he soon became impressed with her—especially when it came to the part about her attempts at defending his son, punching and kicking Frankie. Even though she didn't appreciate Walter for chuckling about it all, an interesting rapport was developing between them.

When Will returned home and walked into the kitchen, he found them laughing and talking like old friends. As Laverne looked up at him, she saw remaining embarrassment on his face. But with a second look, she saw something else, something positive that she couldn't identify.

Laverne stood up and thanked Walter for the coffee and Will walked outside with her. Neither knew what to say to break the ice regarding their cold memory of the night before, but Will finally asked her, "Wanna see my animals?" Glad for anything to distract them from their self-consciousness, she smiled and nodded, following him into the barn.

Will took a baby rabbit out of a cage and handed it to Laverne. She snuggled the bunny under her chin and stroked its soft fur before Will put it back in the pen.

Loosening up, Will told her about each of the animals and explained how he acquired them. Stopping at each cage, he described how he mended their hurts. "I found some of em' crippled and put splints on their wings or legs. Me and Milford nursed a lotta critters back to health."

Laverne was standing close to Will when she teasingly pleaded, "I've got a broken heart. Can you fix that?"

Knowing what broke her heart, Will became serious with remorse. He looked deeply into her eyes and said, "I am so sorry for what happened last night."

Laverne drew closer and gently admitted, "Will, you're my first love. Nothing will ever change that." Then she tilted her chin up, closed her eyes, pursed her lips, and waited for Will to kiss her. A little surprised by his boldness, he didn't hesitate, even placing his arms around her, passionately responding.

While they were kissing, Milford, with little Becky tailing behind, arrived home from church and entered the barn. Milford let out a shriek, "Whoa eee!" and little Becky giggled interrupting the romantic moment.

Although Walter hadn't met Laverne before that morning, the rest of the family knew Laverne from church and from various events at the school, and both children were always glad to see her. Unfortunately for them, Will wasn't in the mood for sharing, so after they said hello and little Becky got a hug from her, he told them to "Skedaddle!"

After they left, the couple sat face to face using hay bales for seats.

Will brought up the subject of the dance again and lamented. "I hate Frankie Ragsdale and his thugs for what they did to me. But they showed me, I'm not the man I want to be." He took a long piece of the straw from the hay bale and leaned over to draw a line on the barn floor dirt. "It was bad for you to see me disgraced like I was last night—but it won't happen again."

Laverne interrupted in an attempt to reassure him there wasn't anything that would change how she felt about him, but he wasn't finished with what he needed to say. She had also intended on sharing what God showed her about forgiving Frankie, but what Will said next left her bewildered.

Taking her hand before he lost his nerve again, Will told her, "I have to go away. And I've been doing a lot of thinking about us. On Tuesday, I'll let you know where I'm going."

They heard Velma ringing the dinner bell before he finished talking. It reminded Laverne that she had promised her mom they would eat their Sunday meal together, and although she wanted to, she couldn't stay to beg more explanation for the words with which Will had scared her.

Before she could leave, Will pulled her back and kissed her again and told her not to worry. "Meet me at Ruth's Café on Tuesday at four o'clock and I'll tell you everything. And there's something I want to give you."

Laverne thought it would be a long wait for the answers she needed to hear, but as she hurried away, she smiled and said she'd be there.

After Laverne left, Will went in the house to wash up for the Sunday meal. The table was already set and Walter was seated. Velma stood at the stove, tasting and then adding more salt to the creamy gravy makings.

When Milford saw Will enter the room, he delightedly announced to his parents, "I saw Will and Laverne kissin' in the barn today!"

Then little Becky began dancing around the table singing, "Will and Laverne, sittin' in a tree...K I S S I N G!"

Seeing the expression on Will's face, Walter hee-hawed. Velma, understanding Will's sensitivity, frowned at her husband, so Walter appeased her saying, "Well...he coulda done worse. I like that little gal. Will, why didn't you tell her to stay and eat with us?"

6

Recruiting Day

Monday came at last, and after finishing his chores around the farm in much less time than usual to the bafflement of Walter, Will put the pedal to the metal of his pickup and headed for town.

With his heart beating so hard he felt like his chest was jumping, Will walked into the Marine recruiting office. He awkwardly walked up to the counter where a clean-cut Marine with an incredibly wide mouth of white teeth smiled at him and asked him to sign-in. Then the oddly exuberant Marine handed him some paperwork and a pen on a clipboard. Will looked around the waiting room for a place to sit and was surprised at seeing his friend Pete, who had been studiously filling out similar papers.

When Pete saw Will, he stood up. They shook hands and foolishly grinned at each other. Will was the first to ask, "What made you decide to enlist?"

Pete answered, "What the hell. If I don't join, I'll probably get drafted. Besides, since I lost my job, Linda went and got engaged to Billy Hedrick, so I'm gettin' outta Dodge. What about you?"

Before Will had a chance to answer, the Recruiting Sergeant opened his office door and called Pete's name.

Left alone, Will filled out the forms, and after a few minutes, Pete opened the office door, kicked his heels together, stood at attention and mockingly saluted Will. "I'm in baby! You're next."

Will sat in a chair opposite the barrel-chested Recruiting Sergeant who was seated at his desk with a list of questions in front of him. The recruitment interview began immediately and the sergeant fired questions at Will. As the questions were answered, the sergeant checked off each one, sometimes making notations on the paper. Before he ended his inquiries, he asked questions about Will's health. "Do you have any physical handicaps such as an old football injury?"

Will held up the little finger on his left hand. "I pretty near lost my little finger in the darn sugar can grinder when I was ten. Luckily, I only cut the end of it. But I'm right-handed anyway, so I guess it doesn't much matter."

The sergeant confirmed that it didn't much matter. Then he questioned Will about his vision, seeming anxious to complete the interview. Other potential applicants had arrived and the recruiter was anxious for this meeting to be completed. He wanted to see the next aspirants and to meet his quota before they changed their minds—as some had been known to do if they waited too long.

Scratching his head, Will admitted, "I'm not cross-eyed and I don't need glasses, but I guess I should tell you...when I look in a mirror, it looks like my right eye is focused up a bit with my left eye focused down."

Looking at his watch, the sergeant stood up and came around his desk and patted Will on the back. "We need Marines with conditions like yours. You can look up in the trees and down the trail at the same time."

Will left the Recruiting office elated that he was officially signed up for the Marines. But his joy shrunk like a pair of cotton socks washed in hot water that evening when he sat down to eat dinner with his family.

After a few bites, Will moved what was left of the pork chop, cooked carrots and scalloped potatoes all around his plate with a fork, while considering how to make the inevitable announcement to his family. He caught his mother watching him fidget so he picked up his glass, gulped his milk and refilled his glass.

Not only did Velma have the reputation of having eyes in the back of her head like mothers seem to have when their kids are naughty, she could read each child's face like a book. She knew something was troubling Will.

Will couldn't put it off any longer. After taking another swallow of milk, he blurted out the information. "I joined the Marines today."

Except for little Becky, the other members of his family silently stared at him in astonishment.

Little Becky, who had quickly processed the fact, piped, "Will...can you get me a medal for show and tell? Mean 'ol Vernon Pitts showed off his uncle's medal of honor at school today—and he got a lotta points from Mrs. Peabody."

Will gave a half smile to his sister and glanced at his dad. Walter's stern face was crimson, and Velma's face had turned pale as she beheld her husband.

Milford had been grinning with admiration and ranted, "Wow! You really did it huh? That's so cool Will."

Will had been looking at his dad's angry demeanor and the distraction caused him to ignore Milford's enthusiasm. He tried to think of something that would get his dad's approval.

Will directed his words at Walter. "The Recruiting Sergeant said I'd be a good point man. And it looks like I'll get to go to a place called Parris Island."

Walter stood up and shoved his chair into the table so hard it caused the dishes to clatter, and the remaining milk in Will's glass spilled out on the checkered tablecloth.

Walter spewed, "You stupid jackass. I hate to burst your bubble, but a Point is the guy who draws enemy fire and is first to be killed in combat. Parris Island is in South Carolina and it used to be a Navy prison. You shouldn't be so damn excited about being sent to Hell."

Velma had nervously wiped up the spilt milk and tears had trickled down her cheeks after Walter left the room. He'd slammed the back screen door so hard that one of the hinges broke. Milford and little Becky were stupefied and stared at their mother.

After a few more uncomfortable minutes, Will left the house and drove away in his pick-up. He had a plan, and he would carry it through come hell or high water.

He needed to meet with Charlie Shipman. If Charlie was willing, he would arrange for Charlie to help Walter on the farm when he left for recruit training. Also, Charlie had shown interest in buying Will's pick-up, and Will needed the money for the purchase he had in mind.

7

Proposal

By Tuesday afternoon, Walter had cooled off somewhat, but things were still tense between him and his son. Velma hadn't said much, but comforted Will by telling him that he was old enough to make his own decisions and she was proud of him for doing that. Jimmy T. had stopped by the farm and praised Will for doing at last what he'd always wanted to do. Milford had already started to make preparations for rearranging the bedroom he would have all to himself, and earlier in the day, little Becky had proudly informed Vernon Pitts that her brother was a Marine and she would be bringing a better medal than his uncle's for show and tell.

Later in the afternoon, after spending almost an hour at Jamie Johns Jewelry Store, Will settled on the ring to buy for Laverne and pulled out the cash to pay for it.

Ruth's Café was only a block away from Jamie Johns, and Will arrived there a few minutes before four o'clock. He sat in a booth in the back corner where he could see anyone coming in the door, and ordered a cup of coffee from the skinny blonde waitress who was Pete's older sister, Sally Springer.

After Sally brought his coffee, she went to the jukebox and punched in a song called, "Soldier Boy" by the Shirelles, and looked back at Will, demurely.

At exactly four o'clock, Laverne entered the café. With piercing eyes, looking straight ahead at the back corner booth, she walked past the café customers who were seated at a dozen green Formica-topped tables, and headed for Will. She plopped down in the seat across from him and glared.

A little scared that he already knew why she was behaving that way, Will asked her, "What's wrong?"

With fiery eyes, Laverne blurted out her response a little too loudly causing a couple of people to turn around and stare, "I don't remember you telling me you were going to join the Marines."

Will tried to reach across the table to grab Laverne's hand, but she withdrew it and looked down. Her mouth turned to a pout. When Sally came to the table to take her order, Laverne, still simmering, hadn't looked up, so Will ordered her a cup of coffee.

With long pauses between his sentences, Will sighed, "I'm sorry. But nobody gets it. It was a decision I had to make...alone. I need you to understand, Laverne."

Laverne was never successful at staying perturbed with Will, and as he explained his reasoning, she quickly weakened. She pulled a handkerchief out of her purse and blew her nose, and at last she looked up at him and muttered, "Oh Will...I kinda understand. It's just...When I heard Charlie telling everybody at work that you and Pete had enlisted, I thought I'd die. It was such a surprise. He said you'll be gone for eleven weeks."

Will banged the table lightly. "Doggone that Charlie. He shoulda let me make my own announcements."

Laverne put her hands on the table, giving Will another opportunity to hold them; however, he didn't take them right away. He wasn't yet ready to take the chance of being denied a second time.

Meanwhile, Sally had brought Laverne a cup of coffee and refilled Will's cup, slyly assessing the situation between the couple. The drama that occurred every day at the café tables was better than the soap operas she watched on her break.

Finally, Laverne reached out for Will's hands to reassure him of her change of heart, then he gave them to her eagerly. For a while they just sat in the booth looking at each other.

Suddenly, Laverne remembered. She sat up very straight and reminded Will excitedly, "You said you had something to give to me today. What is it?"

Will had been waiting for the right moment. He took a deep breath and swallowed. "Laverne, I've made a lot of positive decisions since last week. You are a big part of them because I...I...love you. I know the Marines are going to help me to become what I need to be, and I have to do this...for both of us."

Laverne's eyes glowed as she listened to him and then she admitted, "I've been praying for you, and I guess I should know that God was the one that directed you to enlist. I know He has a plan for us."

Will pleaded, "Laverne, will you wait for me?"

Laverne had never heard Will speak so ardently. She would remember the moment forever. She nodded and smiled, with love radiating from her face.

Then Will reached in his pocket and pulled out a small box and flipped it open to reveal a sparkling engagement ring.

Will asked the question she had waited to hear since she was ten. Placing both hands to her face, Laverne wept with joy.

Taking her hand, Will slipped the ring on her index finger and then moved to the other side of the table and boldly kissed her, not caring a bit who was watching. Enraptured in their embrace, they were oblivious to the people looking at them. But before they stopped kissing, applause was heard throughout the restaurant. Sally had drawn attention to the couple by noting Will's proposal to each of her customers. Everyone in the restaurant, including the cook, was looking at them and clapping their hands.

Then everybody, including Will and Laverne, laughed. When the laughter subsided, Will advised the cheering audience, "You're all the first to know, but don't tell anybody yet, especially Charlie Shipman, or everybody in town will know before my mom!"

8

Departure

Preparations had been completed and the day Will had dreamed about for so long had finally come.

He had sold his pick-up to Charlie Shipman in order to pay for Laverne's engagement ring. On that same day he'd arranged for Charlie to work with his dad at the farm. Charlie needed more part-time work besides his part-time security duty at the Recorder's Office, and Walter was overjoyed after seeing that his new help could probably pull more loads than the mule.

Will was ready. He had packed his suitcase a week before. He and Jimmy T had said their goodbyes the day before, promising to write to each other, and Will had cleared out the bedroom for Milford and boxed up a few possessions to be stored in the barn. He reminded Milford how to care for his remaining animals, after setting free several that had been mended and healed. Will had even worked with Radar, following Charlie's advice in order to housebreak Radar before he left.

The pieces of the puzzle needed for Will's peace of mind before he left the farm had fallen together. In fact, he felt there was relevance with how everything was falling into place because of everybody's prayers. Even his dad was showing a change of heart, and Will had done a little praying himself when he went to church with Laverne.

He was embarrassed when the members of the church gathered around him to pray, but their enthusiastic prayers for his blessing and protection in the adventure that lay ahead, deeply moved him.

On the morning of Will's departure to training camp, Sally Springer drove to the Brown farm in her dad's 1962, two-toned Oldsmobile with her brother, Pete, in the front seat, and Laverne in the backseat. Sally beeped the horn and they waited for Will to say his goodbyes to his family.

Will picked up little Becky and they shared butterfly kisses while she giggled. His mother stood at the kitchen counter with her back to him, sniffling and closing the paper sack she'd prepared with snacks for him on the train. After putting Becky down, Will came up behind Velma, put his arms around her waist and hugged her with emotion. She wiped her eyes with her apron, making Walter uncomfortable with her sentimentality.

Will held his hand out to his dad and they shook hands, without words.

Milford had picked up his brother's suitcase and the paper sack and carried it outside to the car. The rest of the family followed Will outside but remained on the porch where Radar was waiting patiently to get back inside the house.

Will high-fived and hugged his younger brother before he got in the backseat of the car, and everyone waved until the car was on the paved road.

The four Browns slowly walked back into the house with Walter being the last to enter. To Velma's wonder, for the first time in twenty years, Walter hadn't slammed the door.

On the way to the train station, Laverne snuggled up to Will in the back seat and put her head on his shoulder. Sally had the car radio turned up loud as The Lettermen crooned, "When I Fall in Love." The romantic music fit their mood, until Pete started clowning around, theatrically singing along and making everyone laugh.

When they arrived at the station, they saw several families, friends and girlfriends there for the sendoff of other recruits, and a bus with a few recruits from other towns pulled up and emptied.

All the recruits were directed to sign in and board the train immediately. After signing in, Pete hugged his sister and Will tenderly kissed Laverne.

Picking up their suitcases along with the paper sacks each brought, the girls watched them join the group of potential Marines. Inside the train, all the passengers appeared to be near the same age, but there was an assortment of heights, builds and nationalities. The seats were filled with noisy and excited recruits and the air was filled with cigarette smoke.

Laverne's tears spilled out when Will and Pete waved at the girls through the window and the train moved down the tracks.

The train had barely pulled out of the station when Pete slyly unscrewed the top of the whiskey bottle which was in the paper sack he brought. Keeping most of the bottle covered with the brown paper, he held the mouth of the bottle to his lips, swallowed, made a face and then bragged, "This is really living. Thanks to Uncle Sam, this free trip across the country is gonna be like a vacation." He took another swig and held the bottle towards Will. "I brought us a little false courage for the journey."

Will declined the offer. He wasn't interested in the booze, mainly because he didn't want to miss a thing on the adventure for which he had waited for so long. Besides, He was plenty high anticipating the journey set before him.

The whiskey bottle was half empty when Pete recapped the bottle and fell asleep. His mouth hung open and he kept sliding into Will. Will had to push him aside to keep him from laying his head on his shoulder. Finally, Pete's stale whiskey breath was too hard to take, so Will grabbed the bag his mother had prepared with snacks, and moved to another seat on the train to enjoy them.

Will appreciated the camaraderie of other recruits who introduced themselves and wanted to become acquainted; although, he wasn't sure if it was just his mother's oatmeal cookies which interested them.

That evening, the train pulled into the station at Yemassee, South Carolina. The recruits were ushered off the train and into two green Marine Corps buses. Pete was tipsy and tripped on the steps as he was exiting the train. Davis, one of the recruits that Will had met, helped Will grab Pete under his arms and they assisted Pete in moving to the bus as inconspicuously as possible.

After a fifteen minute ride, the buses arrived and parked in front of what looked like an old abandoned church out of a scary Alfred Hitchcock movie. The grounds were poorly lit and surrounded by a barbwire fence with only one strand of barbwire. Two rusted tin signs hung crookedly on the fence and were jangling by a slight wind. The eerie rattling sound contributed to the Hitchcock sensation. The faded signs read: YEMASSEE FIRST SCHOOL and CHURCH OF THE HOLY GHOST.

The passengers in the buses had become quieter as they looked out the windows. Recruit Davis was the first to comment. "This don't look like no Marine Base." A man with tattoos all over his arms added, "This here is some weird shit. Didn't this use to be a grammar school? And I don't think we're here for a church service."

Recruit Ruiz suggested in broken English and Spanish, "Theese must be la iglesia y educacion for espectro!" (This is a church with education for ghosts.)

When the bus doors creaked open, Pete woke up and pulled out his bottle again. He had a few swallows of whiskey so the "hair of the dog" might relieve the beginnings of a headache.

The recruits were ushered into the church yard which was used as a holding area. They were obliged to wait there for an hour because three miles away, a platoon was still in receiving on the island.

Finally, a green, Marine Jeep, roared up the dirt road and parked behind the buses. Three Marines, wearing Smoky Bear hats and carrying clipboards, climbed out of the vehicle and entered the yard authoritatively.

By then, Pete was feeling very loose. Acting like a choir director, he began singing the Marine hymn, drawing the immediate attention of the Drill Instructors. The shortest and meanest looking DI moved towards Pete, whereupon Pete, oblivious to the gravity of the situation, tried to hug him. Faster than a speeding bullet, the irritated DI grabbed the almost empty whiskey bottle from Pete and broke it on a fence post. Then he took Pete by the back of the neck and the seat of his pants and threw him toward the bus. When Pete landed, another DI was there to give him a few kicks in the rear before he flung him inside the bus. In the bus, the third DI seized him and forcefully positioned him in a seat, announcing, "Welcome to Parris Island, asshole."

After brief directions from the short DI, all the recruits were ushered to the bus while the DI's mocked them.

"Let's go girls."

"The bus is waiting for you dickhead."

"Do you have shit for brains?"

"Get movin' elephant ass!"

Will sat beside Pete in the bus. Pete had sobered up considerably, but was still a little fuzzy. He looked up at his friend and simply said, "Oh-oh."

9

Parris Island

The bright lights of the Recruit Depot could be seen glowing from some distance. When they entered the gates, Will noticed the MP's were smiling as they watched the buses pass through. The buses parked in front of a building that had a sign over the entrance that read, RECEIVING.

A Marine sergeant came out of the grey building wearing a Smokey bear hat. After the bus doors creaked open, the recruits heard him commanding. "Fall outside in three ranks and put your feet on the yellow markers."

The recruits moved out of the buses, and after much awkward shuffling, finally settled on the yellow footprint markers and waited for further instructions. No one spoke as the tough-looking DI critically looked over the recruits and yelled with a piercing voice that demanded their complete attention.

The sergeant roared, "You will only speak when spoken to! And every word out of your mouth will be preceded and ended with 'Sir.' This is not a summer camp, Boy Scout camp or home on the range. This is the United States Marine Corps." He approached the recruit who had long, blonde hair and continued bellowing a quarter inch from his face. "Ladies, your lives will be undergoing major changes within these grounds to make you into useful men."

Turning to the overweight recruit who quickly eliminated the smile from his face, the DI thundered, emphasizing each word. "The difficult, we do right away. The impossible takes eleven weeks because it takes eleven weeks to turn whale shit into well-greased killing machines."

For fifteen minutes, the recruits stood on the yellow footprints while instruction regarding the details to follow that night were harshly conveyed. Two MP's stood on the sidelines with their arms crossed and their feet apart, amused as they watched the new recruits, some of whom looked scared enough to pee their pants.

Pete and Will were standing on the yellow footprints in the back row. Thinking he wouldn't be heard, Pete murmured to Will, "Why is this S O B so pissed off?"

The recruits were marched single file into the first station where ten, grinning, masochistic barbers waited to shave their heads. The lighting was especially bright and the clean shaved heads glowed as they were moved to the second station.

In the second station, they were ordered to speedily remove everything they wore and box whatever they brought with them.

All the recruits moved stark naked and self-consciously to the third station where they walked barefooted through a shallow trough of disinfectant for their feet. From there, they moved directly to the showers.

In the fourth station, they were efficiently issued Marine utilities and clothing, including underwear, boots, cap, belt and a laundry bag to carry all the items.

Hygiene items were issued in the fifth station including towels and wash cloths.

Still conspicuously naked and uncomfortable, the goose-bumped recruits were ordered to move to the sixth station where medical personnel inspected each individual, and then inoculated them with several shots.

Finally, to their relief, they were ushered into a large area where they were ordered to get dressed and fall outside in three ranks. Then dressed in stiff, though surprisingly well-fitting clothing, the recruits were marched through the base to an area that had a dozen World War II Quonset Huts. They had been told that due to the large number of enlistments and draftees, the new barracks were full.

The three ranks were halted in front of the Quonset Huts that would be their permanent quarters for eleven weeks. Inside, a Drill Instructor sternly ordered them to place their folded towels on the left side of the foot of their beds, and their laundry bags on the right side. Then he ordered them to make their beds and "Hit the sack" when the taps sounded.

There were double bunks, each with two sheets, a pillow, a pillow case and a blanket. A metal identification card holder was at the foot of each bed. It had been a long day, and the simple bunk beds inside the huts looked pretty good to the exhausted recruits. The recruits barely had enough time to make their beds before taps sounded.

Pete was in the bunk above Will's. He leaned his head over the edge and whispered, "What in the hell did we get ourselves into? Have you ever in your life seen such insane, sadistic human beings? I'd rather face the fucking sharks than stay on this island." While Pete was still carrying on, he finally realized he'd been talking to himself because Will was asleep.

At four in the morning, Will was dreaming that he was still kissing Laverne goodbye at the train station. Awakened by the noise of someone taping on his bunk, he discovered it was only the pillow he smooched. Still half asleep with his eyes closed, he wondered why the rooster hadn't crowed yet. Then remembering where he was, he opened his eyes and squinted as someone turned on all the overhead lights.

A midget Marine was standing beside his bed. He had short, bright red hair and was beating the end of his bunk with a swagger stick. The elfin Marine was clothed in a miniature green Marine uniform and he looked at Will sternly. In a little child's shrieking voice he audaciously yelled, "Fall outside!"

As Will sat up and rubbed his eyes, trying to figure out if he was still dreaming, the Senior Drill Instructor, Staff Sergeant Kohler, who also had red hair, added in a much lower and authoritative voice, "You heard him. Outside in three ranks!" Meanwhile, to make sure everyone was awake, two other Drill Instructors had been banging their nightsticks on the garbage cans outside the Quonset Hut.

Will heard sleepy, negative declarations coming from the bunk above him as he was quickly getting dressed. All the recruits were scrambling except one. He pulled the pillow out from under Pete's head, encouraging him to get up, then Will finished dressing and tore out the door.

Hung-over and yawning, Pete was the last to line up outside, still stuffing his shirt in his pants, seconds before the DI Sergeant reappeared.

The Marine child stood proudly beside Sergeant Kohler as the dignified sergeant made introductions in an icy voice.

"I am Staff Sergeant Kohler. This is my son, Victor. You will also become acquainted with Sergeant Jakobowski and Sergeant Wrobelski who will be assisting me for the next eleven weeks. You will remember that anytime you wish to speak to us it will be preceded by 'Sir' and will end with 'Sir.' Is that understood?"

The platoon responded. "Sir, yes Sir."

Kohler continued, "Reveille will be at four-thirty a.m. You will have fifteen minutes to shit, shave, shower and shampoo; thirty minutes to get in and out of the chow hall; fifteen minutes to make your beds, clean your quarters, dress and be outside in three ranks by five-thirty. Is that understood?"

The platoon responded. "Sir, yes Sir."

Kohler continued, "Your beds will be made with hospital folds at all four corners, with a six inch fold from the head."

As he gave directions, Kohler had stood solidly in one place while informing the recruits. But then, announcing further stipulations, he moved around in front of them, steadily looking into their faces, confirming the strength behind his orders with eyes and demeanor that chilled.

"There will be no grab-ass, you will not flog your mule or spank you monkey while you are here. You will not smoke, chew gum, eat pogey bait or drink soda pop. You will not use racial slurs, lie or steal. You will memorize your twelve general orders and recite them on request."

"If you are a Christian, Islamic, Jew, Buddhist or religious person you may pray to the God of your choice. But at five-thirty every morning, your natural ass belongs to me! Is that understood?"

The platoon responded. "Sir, yes Sir."

Kohler continued, "In the next eleven weeks, you will be born again in spirit, soul and body. The umbilical to your former self will be severed and you will be trans-formed!"

10

The Transformation Begins

Sergeant Kohler had been making notes on his clipboard while Drill Instructors, Sergeant Jakobowski and Sergeant Wrobelski stood in front of the recruits. Jakobowski was rapidly hollering orders.

"Face to the right and cover down according to height. If the person in front of you is shorter, move ahead of him."

After some confusion in figuring out where each person belonged, the tallest individuals stood in the front with more than a foot difference in heights from those in the back.

Then Jakobowski yelled. "Face to the left! When Sergeant Wrobelski stops in front of you, state your name and where you're from."

Each recruit obediently responded with the requested information as the intimidating, muscular Wrobelski looked at each of them with contempt. Moving towards Pete, he stopped in front of him.

"Sir, Pete Springer, Beckley, West Virginia, Sir."

The DI remained in front of him, and sniffed the air. "Private Springer, are you wearing perfume?"

"Sir, no Sir."

Sniffing again, the DI screeched his opinion. "You smell sweet. You have a feminine voice and a fair complexion. Your smell and your voice betray you, and your beer belly doesn't fit with your skinny legs. You should be transferred to the WM's."

Pete knew he'd put on a few pounds after he lost his job at the Sav-A-Lot market. With nothing to do while he waited for induction, he'd been spending a lot of time at Ruth's Café, eating and drinking more than usual. He asked the sergeant, "Sir, what's a WM, Sir?"

Koehler's son, Victor, dressed in his little green uniform, was on the base for the day, and hearing Pete's question, had stopped riding his tiny bike on the sidewalk nearby. Wrobelski sardonically assigned Victor to respond to Pete's question.

Getting off his bike and putting his hands on his hips, the child informed Pete. "The WM's is for the girl recruits on this island."

Wrobelski and Jakobowski walked down the three ranks and ordered overweight recruits to move to the bus boarding area and get on the bus with the sign "MOTIVATION" in the destination window. Meanwhile, Sergeant Kohler elaborated.

"Those of you who are obviously overweight and need an attitude adjustment are going to Motivation Platoon. You will find there is no smorgasbord at Motivation Platoon. It is a secluded area, off limits to civilians, including the press who are curious about the rumors spread regarding Marine torture. The recruits will not be harassed but concentrate on diet and physical training."

All the new recruits were pressed hard every day in instruction and discipline, separating the men from the boys. Along with the others, Will Brown fell into the strict Marine routines, while feeling a sense of unity with his brother recruits. Pursuing his goal to be a better person, he used all his power to stretch himself to the DI's demands, finding stamina and strength which he didn't know he had. And although much of what was required was repetitive, each day he learned something new with seemingly endless drills and information to process. For instance, the Drill Instructors taught the recruits what they called Close Order Drill including right face, left face, open ranks, parade rest, right step, count off, quick time, double time, left and right flank, oblique, about face, left turn, right turn and attention. Over and over again, the recruits responded to the tedious commands until they got them right.

A Marine had shouted, "Attention!" DI Sergeant Kohler carried out a small red flag on a pole. The guidon, which was the identification of the military unit, had the words Platoon 101 in gold print. The DI assigned recruit Jeffries as the honored position of Guidon Bearer. Then Kohler commanded, "Platoon, fall in, right face, forward march. Let me see what you've got. Double time. March!" When he screamed, "March," it always sounded like "Harch."

Kohler ran the platoon hard for one mile, but some fell out breathing hard and others fell out vomiting. Only fifteen men finished the mile at the first attempt.

The DI's ran the platoon every morning until all fifty stayed with them. The platoon was taught to chant to keep their minds off their suffering.

Although the meter wasn't perfect, chanting served a purpose—and it was often entertaining:

DI: "Look to the right and what did I pass?"
Platoon: "Look to the right and what did I pass?"
DI: "An ugly recruit with a big fat ass."
Platoon: "An ugly recruit with a big fat ass."
DI: "You'll run five miles as part of the plan."
Platoon: "You'll run five miles as part of the plan."
DI: "To make your self one tough young man."
Platoon: "To make your self one tough young man."
DI: "You love lima beans, but odors they bring."
Platoon: "You love lima beans, but odors they bring."
DI: "It's not becomin' for a U.S. Marine."
Platoon: "It's not becomin' for a U.S. Marine."
DI: "They give you gas and make you fart."
Platoon: "They give you gas and make you fart."
DI: "But better than a whore who'll break your heart."
Platoon: "But better than a whore who'll break your heart."
DI: "Prettiest girl I ever seen."
Platoon: "Prettiest girl I ever seen."
DI: "Dressed in blue and sweet sixteen."
Platoon: "Dressed in blue and sweet sixteen."
DI: "I'm gonna ask her to be my queen."
Platoon: "I'm gonna ask her to be my queen."

On Armory Day, in the second week of training, the recruits were issued rifles and 782 gear which included a helmet, cartridge belt, canteen and bayonet. Then Sergeant Kohler warned, "You will keep your rifle cleaner than your body. You will memorize your rifle number, and if your rifle is found dirty, you will sleep with it until graduation." With an intense expression on his face he added solemnly, "The most lethal combination in the world is a Marine and his rifle."

Later, the same day, Sergeant Jakobowski and Sergeant Wrobelski painstakingly taught the recruits the Manual of Arms including right shoulder arms, left shoulder arms, port arms, present arms and order arms. Eventually, they also taught the Marching Manual.

That night on his bunk, Will read a letter he received at mail call. It was from his brother, Milford and as he read, he began laughing hysterically. When Pete asked him what was so funny, Will read a portion of the letter. "Everybody has been missing you and acting weird. Even Radar has been behaving crazy. He rubs his nose in his own crap. Then he chews up the newspaper and jumps out the window."

Pete didn't laugh and said, "I don't get it."

Will explained how he'd tried to train Radar according to Charlie Shipman's instructions. Then seeing that Pete was not entertained and looked downcast, he asked him how he was doing.

Pete sighed, "Well at least they finally gave us a rifle. Of course, if they don't feed me somethun' more than low calorie/high protein meals, I'm not sure I'll have the strength to carry it."

Will nudged, "Aw come on Pete, you're already lookin' better than when you got here. Don't you feel better than you did sittin' around eating greasy cheeseburgers and drinkin' chocolate malts at Ruth's Café?"

Pete wailed, "Ohhh...I can't think about it," put his pillow over his head and lay on his bunk with a noisy stomach growling until he fell asleep.

The following day was a brutal day of Grinder-Close-Order drilling. Sergeant Kohler bellowed specific commands for over an hour. "Platoon, ten-hut-right-face-right-shoulder-arms-forward. Harch! Settle down, you're bouncing like a fat lady's tits. Forty inches back to breast, look to your right and get your dress. Dig in your heels! Glance out the right corner of your eye and keep in line. I said...keep in line!"

A recruit from Florida named Driscoll, suddenly stopped, utterly frustrated. Dragging his rifle in dismay, he walked out of the ranks, emotionally distraught. Kohler immediately turned the platoon over to Sergeant Jakobowski and Sergeant Wrobelski and ordered Driscoll to go over and sit down under a tree by the curb, which was some distance from the platoon. Analyzing Driscoll's appearance, Kohler sat down on the curb next to him and remained silent for a moment. His prideful goal of making a good Marine out of every recruit was a challenge. Yet always, somehow, he'd do it!

Kohler began slowly. "Driscoll, did you know I was raised on a farm in central Florida by my Grandparents? There was no electricity and we had to carry water from a hand pump in the yard. The privy was a two holer outside and we used a Sears catalog for toilet paper."

As the sergeant spoke, Driscoll finally looked up at him with some semblance of identifying with him—which was the sole purpose of Kohler's creative story. The fabrication continued.

"It was a tough time for me, but I learned something from it. One day our mule fell in an old well. We tried everything we knew to do to get him out and couldn't. So, Granddaddy said, 'We done all we could do,' so we had to bury him there."

"We started shoveling dirt on him. That mule just kept shakin' it off. And you know, the very thing that would have buried him...he used to walk free."

Driscoll blew his nose and looked at the DI.

"Driscoll, I believe the Marines would lose a good man if they gave you your walking papers. What effect would that have on your family and your self-confidence? It's going to get easier, so why don't you be like that mule, get this shit under your feet and graduate?"

At last, Driscoll got his emotions under control. He picked up his rifle, and saluted Kohler. "Yes Sir. Thank you Sir." Then the sergeant sent him back to the platoon, double time.

Kohler sat on the curb and watched him, then talking to himself said, "You silver-tongued bastard."

Despite what everyone endured, there never seemed to be a shortage of laughter on the base. Probably because after a hard day of physical and mental training, laughter was somewhat of a survival technique. Crying was unacceptable and complaining showed weakness. Complaints were voiced, but they were spoken implicitly in the form of humor.

Some of the recruits had never been away from home before their induction, and homesickness was common. The end of the day offered an outlet for inner anxieties to be dealt with through joking around.

That evening on the way back to their quarters, Recruit Collins grimly whispered to his new friends, "Did you hear about the dead, naked Marine that washed up on Myrtle Beach? There was no way to identify him."

Will fell for the joke and questioned, "Come on Collins, how'd they know he was a Marine if he was naked and had no ID?" Collins gloated as he spoke the punch line. "He had his ass chewed out."

Recruit Davis decided to take his turn at telling a story. "Sergeant Jakobowski said in the old corps, they played horseshoes with the horses still on them." And as always, Pete couldn't resist adding something for his buddies to laugh about. "You know what finally convinced that sissy to use his parachute and jump out of an airplane? Flying at fifteen thousand feet with three dead engines." The jokes continued inside the Quonset hut, but when the lights were out and taps played, the tired recruits slept.

Reveille sounded at 4:30 as usual. One hour later, after the recruits had received large portions of warm oatmeal slopped into a bowl at the chow line, they stood outdoors at attention in their usual positions. The sun hadn't come up and the air was cool and clean. The high tide made the Atlantic Ocean waves pound higher up the beach with a nice sound.

Sergeant Kohler was doing a surprise rifle inspection, and just as he approached Pete Springer, a sand flea had crawled up Springer's nose. Pete had been making every effort towards good behavior and remaining at attention. He was still sore from the last discipline when he was forced to do extra pushups. But the flea brought tears to his eyes as it stung him, and he tried to inconspicuously blow it out of his nose. With a raised eyebrow, Kohler could see what was happening and silently watched him for a while before he quipped, "Springer, you've had your breakfast haven't you?"

Pete answered as a tear stole down his cheek, "Sir, yes Sir." Kohler smirked, "Now let him have his."

11

Marine Classroom

After the thorough rifle inspection, the recruits were marched to a gray building for classroom instruction. Inside the starkly lighted building, the United States Marine insignia, the American flag and three photographs were displayed on the front wall. The three large photographs were pictures of the Former President Dwight D. Eisenhower, the late President John F. Kennedy and the current President, Lyndon B. Johnson.

The recruits stood at attention in front of rows of desks accommodated with paper and pencils for note taking. They sat when the ominous Sergeant Kohler finally said, "At ease," and severely warned them, "You will learn the information we are going to give you in this room. There will be several sessions including 'History and Traditions of the Marines' and 'Code of Conduct.'"

"First, you will remember the Marine's motto is Semper Fidelis which in Latin means 'Always Faithful.' The Marine emblem, as you see displayed with the eagle, globe and anchor signifies that Marines serve our nation, worldwide and sea. Marines are twenty percent of the Navy. We abide by Navy regulations and submit to the Secretary of The Navy."

"You will familiarize yourself with aboard ship terminology including: Deck for floor; bulkhead for wall; head for bathroom, overhead for ceiling; chow for food; port for left; starboard for right; swab for mop; brig for jail and scuttlebutt for gossip."

Sergeant Kohler was a domineering, arrogant, fear-inspiring man to the recruits, but he was also an exceptional DI who served and loved his country. On the following days in the classroom, there was no doubt that Kohler found the Marine facts of history to be hallowed details as he solemnly related them. He began with what he considered most notable, but eventually, he thoroughly elaborated on all of the Marine Corps history.

"On November 10, 1775, in Philadelphia, Pennsylvania, a group of men in the smoky, sailor's hangout called Tuns Tavern, became the first recruits for the Marine Corps. The fact is, they were lured into service with the promise of free grog."

"The oldest weapon still in use by US forces is the Mameluke Sword worn by Marine officers. It was presented to Lieutenant Presley O'Banion by Hamid, the American candidate for the throne in Tripoli."

"In 1820, the Marine uniform featured a high leather collar to protect the jugular vein when in combat. Now you know why Marines have been called 'Leathernecks.'"

"In 1847, the Marines assaulted the citadel of Chapultepec, the Halls of Montezuma in Mexico. The red stripe on the trousers of the dress blue uniform signifies the blood shed at Chapultepec."

"In 1918, the Marines fought the Germans so ferociously in Belleau Woods, the Germans named them 'Teufelhunden' after the legendary devil dog."

"After the Japanese attacked Pearl Harbor on December 7, 1941, the Marines fought up the chain of islands, Guadalcanal, Tarawa, Iwo Jima, Bougainville, Peleliu, Guam and Saipan."

"There were more than five thousand Marine casualties and sixty thousand Japanese casualties in seventeen days of fighting over eight square miles of volcanic ash on Iwo Jima alone."

"Admiral Chester Nimitz said, 'After the Marines took Iwo and planted the flag on Mount Surabachi, uncommon valor was a common virtue.'"

Kohler paused and looked seriously at the class. Then he admonished, "Never forget the price that was paid to give you the honor of wearing the Marine uniform and the privilege to be called Marines."

Will Brown had listened attentively to everything that Koehler taught. Unlike many of the recruits, Will already knew most of the facts that the DI related. He'd spent his high school years learning about the Marines in his longing to have a place with them. Of course, his dreams were different than what he'd experienced so far in the harsh reality of boot camp; nevertheless, he had no regrets.

After another thirty minutes of teaching, Kohler asked several individuals questions to see if they were really listening and retaining the information. Will was one of the recruits who answered all questions correctly. Impressed with him, yet tainted with DI sarcasm, Kohler announced, "Brown, you are a phenomenon of intelligence."

Will couldn't stop the color that he felt rising to his face, and he knew he'd be certain to receive teasing about Kohler's comment by the other men.

And sure enough, as Pete Springer and recruit Johnson sat on Johnson's bunk and played Scrabble that evening, Pete yelled, "Hey Will, T-o-l-e ain't a word is it?"

Will replied, "I don't think tole is a word. How would you use it? I tole you so?"

The men who were listening chuckled. Then Johnson responded, "Okay Brown, you phenomenon of intelligence...haven't you ever heard of a tole bridge?"

Just as Will anticipated, he was the joke of the day and everyone laughed some more. He decided to agree with Johnson, even though he knew how to spell toll bridge. He winked at his audience and conceded, "You can't argue with tole bridge, Pete."

Sergeant Jakobowski taught the Conduct Class later in the week. After showing an old video which showed interviews of former Marine soldiers who had been imprisoned in other countries during war, Jakobowski began instruction.

"The Code of Conduct is the legal guide for behavior if you are captured by hostile forces."

"During the Korean conflict, American servicemen faced something they had never faced before. It has been called, 'Brain Warfare.' When the enemy took prisoners, they isolated them and only gave them negative information. If they received letters, they were only given letters with things that could discourage them such as death of a family member, Dear John letters or bad news of any kind. Prisoners were never given letters that were sent from their family about a birth, good news or ones indicating someone was praying for them."

"They existed in desperation, month after month in darkness without hope. In some cases the prisoners became so despondent, they curled up in the fetal position and died without a mark on them."

"So, the Code of Conduct had to be changed so that the enemy cannot harm you with your personal information. You need to understand how to evade answering anything that would hurt you, your family or your country to the utmost of your ability. Any questions?"

Pete Springer raised his hand. "Sir, what does 'to the utmost' mean, Sir?"

Jakobowski replied, "Springer, if they put your balls in a vice, somewhere between round and flat would be to the utmost. Is that clear now?"

Pete gulped and nodded. After the DI finished elaborating on the Code of Conduct, the recruits were dismissed to join Sergeant Wrobelski. "Outside, on the double, for a little exercise."

The tedious calisthenics lasted over an hour. One of the recruits complained, "It would be easier to swim across the Atlantic Ocean than participate in Wrobelski's idea of a 'little exercise'". He was immediately told to "Shut up!" by several individuals who understood that in the past, smart-mouthed individuals had brought further torture to everyone else—and it was definitely too cool for swimming.

Before the recruits rested, they were ordered to begin doing sit-ups as fast as humanly possible for three minutes. While they were still sitting on the ground recovering, breathing fast and sweating, they were told what they would be doing for class the next day.

"Tomorrow you will become more familiarized with your M14 Rifle, the rifle weight, muzzle velocity, effective range and specific facts, including the fact that it is a gas operated, semi-automatic shoulder weapon. You will learn to fire the weapon for qualification and be taught to field strip the M14 in ten seconds, blindfolded. More of your class time will be spent learning about your rifle than any other subject."

That night before lights out, Will Brown and Pete Springer talked about how much they had already changed since they arrived at Parris Island.

Pete bragged as he flexed his arms, "Look at this muscle, brother. I never thought I could look so good in such a short time. And I haven't starved to death like I thought I would just eatin' all them vegetables. Wait till Linda sees me. 'Betcha she'll dump Billy Hedrick when I get back home."

Will asked, "I thought you said she was already engaged to him."

Pete nodded, "Yeah, but just wait 'till she sees the fabulous, new, irresistible me!"

Will snickered and agreed that she would be impressed. He added quietly, "I think we're both becoming the men we need to be. I only hope Laverne will wait for me like she said she would. I got a letter from her that said Frankie Ragsdale has been pesterin' her. He even asked her out. With all his money, maybe she could be tempted."

50

Pete encouraged, "Are you kidding? Laverne would never go out with that creep. But you know sooner or later, you're gonna have to deal with that asshole."

After the M14 Rifle class was over a few days later, Sergeant Kohler was running the platoon at port arms, chanting whatever came to his mind, often without cadence for the recruits to repeat.

DI: "Jesus, Jesus hear my plea."
Platoon: "Jesus, Jesus hear my plea."
DI: "This DI is killing me."
Platoon: "This DI is killing me."
DI: "Without the pain there ain't no gain."
Platoon: "Without the pain there ain't no gain."
DI: "We may be foul mouthed and obscene."
Platoon: "We may be foul mouthed and obscene."
DI: "But give us a rifle and two canteens."
Platoon: "But give us a rifle and two canteens."
DI: "And we'll show you a killing machine."
Platoon: "And we'll show you a killing machine."

The first day on the obstacle course was a day of exhibiting strength and endurance. The course included forty feet of double tires; a twelve foot balancing plank; a horizontal ladder; a rope climb; a twenty foot wall; a rope swing over water and a crawl tunnel under barbwire. After their acrobatic feats were finally completed, the recruits were required to run a stretch of three hundred yards.

Each day of training was producing the results that Sergeant Kohler had hoped to see. Late one afternoon he watched in appreciation as the platoon marched at right shoulder arms, looking sharp.

DI: "Forty inches back to breast, look to the right and get your dress... Sound off!"
Platoon: "One two."
DI: "Sound off!" Platoon: "Three four."
DI: "Sound off!" Platoon: "One two...Three Four"

12

Survival Techniques

About the time the recruits thought they were mastering things at last and nothing worse could be expected of them, Sergeant Kohler announced it would be Gas Mask Training Day.

Gas masks were distributed and all the recruits were assembled in a circle on the outer perimeter inside a huge tent. Two green, fifty-five gallon drums were placed in the center of the tent. Sergeant Jakobowski ordered everyone to put on their gas masks and begin walking in a circle.

As the recruits began moving, Sergeant Wrobelski dropped tear gas canisters into the drums. As the tear gas was expelled, Jakobowski yelled, "Remove your mask and sing the Marine Hymn."

The tear gas immediately began to irritate the mucous membranes of the recruits eyes, nose, mouth and lungs. Few words from the hymn were articulated before the recruits ran out of the tent with their eyes watering, and most of them were either coughing, sneezing or vomiting.

Without compassion, Jakobowski and Wrobelski waited for the recruits to recover, and then ordered them to the showers.

Before the day was over, the recruits were measured for dress green and khaki uniforms in the Tailor Shop. Including Pete Springer, some of their measurements had changed since induction.

One day when Sergeant Kohler was running the platoon at Port Arms, he stopped them to observe the legendary DI, "Locker Box Jones," who was teaching his platoon the Manual of Arms. A strange sight to see, instead of rifles, they were carrying empty locker boxes. And "Locker Box Jones" was calling out, "Right shoulder locker boxes. Left shoulder locker boxes. Port locker boxes."

As they passed, Kohler noted, "Jones' platoon has never won Honor Platoon, but they always graduate the most buffed out."

On CPR class day, a new and somewhat inexperienced Navy Corpsman instructor was appointed to teach the recruits. Because there weren't enough male upper torso training aids available, the instructor had found a number of female upper torsos for training in order for each individual to learn CPR at the same time. The recruits who were accustomed to the more disciplinary DIs, were having a lot of fun.

One recruit was nursing at the plastic breast instead of blowing in the mouth as instructed. Several others had their hands on each breast instead of pressing down on the sternum, and still others were kissing and turning the torsos every which way, some with goofy looks of ecstasy on their faces. Laughing hysterically at each other, the recruits themselves were close to needing resuscitation.

Sergeant Kohler walked into the building to check on the progress of the class and soberly witnessed the performances. Quickly walking back outside, unable to contain his own amusement, he almost bumped into Sergeant Jakobowski who was peeking in the door and grinning. Kohler looked up at Jakobowski and lamented, "Dear Lord, we've been handed a platoon of sex maniacs."

On the second day of CPR class, the recruits were not so playful, due to the fact that Kohler had made them do more sit-ups than usual because of their disrespect towards the new instructor.

After they learned the correct procedure for CPR, the Navy Corpsman attempted to familiarize the recruits with syringes and self-injections.

"Each of you will be issued a syringe filled with a harmless liquid. Each of you will inject himself like this."

The instructor took a syringe and stabbed himself in the leg, leaving the syringe hanging. One tough-looking, muscular, two hundred and thirty-five pound recruit named Parker, was standing in the first row. Watching the action of the instructor, he turned white and fainted.

Others who were squeamish, closed their eyes or gritted their teeth, but eventually all injected themselves.

One night, a Recruit who had been nicknamed "Hippie," who had long brown hair before the Marine barbers got to him, was seen generously rubbing a smelly substance on his bald head. This was his routine in the showers every night for the past week.

Finally, withholding his curiosity no longer, Recruit Ruiz asked, "Hippie, what have you been rubbing on your cabeza every night?"

Hippie held up the tube of ointment that was almost gone. "It's a new thing that Sergeant Jakobowski told me about. He said it would make my hair grow faster."

Pete Springer overheard the conversation and threw a wet wash cloth at Hippie. "That's Preparation H, asshole."

Pugil Stick Training Day was a comparatively lighthearted time of playfulness for most of the recruits. They were given protective helmets with nose guards, body padding and a pugil stick with padding on the end for increased safety.

The instructor explained what they were to do. "Some of you have never been involved in contact sports. This training is to teach you to be aggressive. You will not retreat at any time. Now line up twenty-five on each side of the combat ring. Those on my left will be the Blue Team, those on my right will be the Red Team. You will battle one another for one full minute."

The first two opponents were ordered into the ring and fought each other with bulldog tenacity. The instructor blew his whistle when the minute was up, they stopped fighting as instructed, and the next opponents went into the ring. This process was repeated until all the recruits had the opportunity to fight.

Most of the men were instinctively aggressive in combat; however, a few of the recruits needed more training. Those that failed to defend and assert themselves were given more chances to fight until the instructor was satisfied with their efforts.

Will Brown was not naturally aggressive, but his experience in dealing with troublesome animals with sharp claws and teeth that had intruded on the farm back home had helped to prepare him somewhat. Still, he had a tendency to back off when his opponent became more forceful. Will's previous experiences with animals and rifles helped him more with Bayonet training Day.

The instructor told the class that bayonet fighting included certain things. "Bayonet fighting involves peripheral vision, moving to keep the enemy in front of you, maintaining a good defense and a good offense at the same time."

Will had already learned those four necessary facts on the farm. But he still had to learn proper stance, left parry, right parry, short thrust, long thrust, horizontal butt stroke, vertical butt stroke, low block, high block, slash and smash.

Lastly, the recruits practiced their loud banshee or rebel yell which frightened the seagulls which frequented the island. The DI explained that a ferocious sounding scream would have a psychological effect on the enemy.

Sergeant Kohler was in charge of Water Survival Day. The indoor swimming pool wasn't heated and the weather had been cold; so the recruits, especially the non-swimmers, weren't looking forward to this experience. Nevertheless, Kohler barked orders that were immediately followed.

"Those of you who don't know how to swim will report to the instructor on the other side of the pool. Recruits that know how to swim will line up, four abreast. When I blow my whistle, dive in, swim the length of the pool and return."

Pete Springer decided to line up with those who knew how to swim. He remembered always having fun skinny-dipping with his friends in the pond, back home in West Virginia, but he forgot that back then, his feet could always reach the bottom of the pond.

Pete was in the first group to dive in. Along with three other recruits, he dove in and started swimming to the distant end of the pool, but the three swimmers soon passed him. Long before he got to the edge, he started sinking. As he began having trouble he yelled, "I can't make it back. I can't make it!"

Kohler grabbed a fifteen foot aluminum pole with a boxing glove on the end and held it out to Pete. Pete reached for it, but instead of rescuing him, Kohler pounded his head three times and calmly shouted, "Swim or drown, Springer."

The other recruits watched in amazement as Pete appeared to be going under. But at last, he began to move his arms in a steady rhythm and made his way to the edge of the pool.

The following day, the recruits, were ordered to climb a twenty-foot tower that represented the side of a ship, located at one end of the swimming pool. Wearing only their trousers, the DI commanded them to jump off the tower, remove their trousers, tie a knot at the end of each leg, grab their trousers by the waist and swoop it over their heads so that air would fill each leg. This training was to teach the recruits to make their trousers a floating device that could be used in an emergency.

This task was not as easy as it seemed and it was a sight to behold. First of all, some of the recruits were not comfortable being on the top of a 20 foot tower, particularly the ones who had only learned to swim the day before. And some required a little persuasion to jump—which was readily provided by accommodating, enthusiastic DI's at the top of the tower. When the recruits hit the water, it took some time to remove their pants that stuck to their bodies. As they struggled to get out of them, it looked like an amateur water ballet performance with their acrobatic moves displaying pointed toes and bare butts making the DI's laugh over the spectacle.

13

Life Lessons

Kohler occasionally took a more personal interest in recruits that appeared to be especially dedicated or teachable. One evening he sent for Will Brown to come to the Senior Drill Instructor's Quarters. Will arrived and knocked on Kohler's door.

Kohler gruffly responded, "Who's knocking on my door?"

"Sir, Recruit Brown, reporting as ordered, Sir."

Kohler said, "Enter."

Will found the DI sitting at his desk, closing the centerfold of a Playboy Magazine. The magazine had recently been confiscated from one of the recruits. Kohler slipped the magazine into the top drawer of his desk and told Will, "At ease Brown. Have a seat." Then He picked up a file that was laying on top of his desk. "I see you're from West Virginia."

Will nodded. "Sir, yes Sir."

Kohler continued, "Why did you enlist in the Corps, Brown?"

"Sir, I didn't like the person I was, Sir."

It was a humble answer that Kohler liked to hear, but rarely heard from recruits. Many men gave the parroted answer, "To serve my country." Although this was an honorable reason, the truth of why they enlisted was often different. He knew a lot of young men whose ultimate purpose for joining was merely to escape something. Bad relationships, broken hearts, poor home life, lack of a job and a myriad of reasons eventually were revealed. Nevertheless, they found new direction, integrity and purposefulness established through the Corps.

Kohler saw Will's sincerity as Will told his story. He listened attentively at how he had been bullied since grammar school, how Frankie Ragsdale had humiliated him in front of his girlfriend, and how he had always wanted to be the man he felt the Marines could help make him.

"So," questioned Kohler, "Ultimately, what kind of a person do you want to be?"

"Sir, I want to be a man with courage. I want to have the strength to be ready, not only for the responsibility I'm given as a Marine, but also for being a husband and a father. I want to be a person who is respected and fearless, Sir."

The DI scratched his head and thought for a moment before he commented. "Brown, first, respect is always earned – and never ordered. As for the Ragsdales of this world, like the poor, you'll always have them."

Will remembered what Jesus said in the Bible. His mother had taught him the verse from Scripture. *For you have the poor with you always, but Me you do not have always.* (Matthew 26:11 NKJV).

He wondered if Kohler read the *Bible* along with his *Playboy Magazine*. He was a curious individual, and as tough as he'd seen him behave, there was also a warmth that he was beginning to see in him.

Kohler continued, "I've noticed that you can be somewhat aggressive with the pugil stick, yet you aren't assertive in other areas. Fear is not only the enemy of Marines, fear is the spiritual enemy of the human race. It is one thing to be tempted by fear, but it's quite another thing to be controlled by fear. Let me ask you, have you ever been in a bare knuckled fist fight with another man?"

Clenching his fist, Will was thinking, someday Ragsdale would feel his fist—but he had to answer Kohler honestly. "No."

Then, standing up and turning his back to Will, Kohler seemed to be looking at the map behind his desk. Finally he spoke, "Brown, I don't make this a habit, but meet me here at 1800 tomorrow night. I'm going to introduce you to a different world."

As requested, Will met Sergeant Kohler the following night. He was surprised to find Kohler dressed in civilian clothes. He was wearing cowboy boots, jeans and a blue and yellow striped western shirt with shiny pearl buttons. Acting secretively, he had looked both ways out the door when Will arrived. Then Kohler told him to wait inside until he pulled up in his car. When he drove the car to the front, he got out of the car and opened the trunk, motioning for Will to get in. Figuring he better do what the sergeant said, Will pressed his body down into the car trunk and Kohler shut the lid.

Two miles down the highway, the car stopped and the trunk was opened. Bewildered, Will climbed out and Kohler handed him a red, long sleeved western shirt and a cowboy hat and told him to put them on. Then he got in the front seat of the car with Kohler and they moved on down the road.

After about an hour of driving, Will saw a neon sign over a building on the right side of the highway that read, BLUE GOOSE. Kohler parked the car, and the incognito sergeant and his recruit walked to the building entrance. A roped off boxing ring was situated outside the bar, a few steps from the door. It served as a practical reminder that the owner of the establishment wanted clients to settle disputes outside rather than tear up the bar.

Except for the fact that the floor was covered with peanut shells instead of pieces of straw, the inside of the place sort of reminded Will of the inside of the barn, back home. People were dancing to a loud Merle Haggard record playing on the Jukebox. Smoke filled the air of the dimly lighted room and Kohler and Will found a table. A few people greeted Kohler like they were old friends and the waitress appeared especially delighted to see him.

Kohler grabbed the short waitress who looked older than anyone in the room, picked her up, swung her around and planted a kiss on the top of her head. Then he introduced her to Will. "Pearl, this is one of my recruits, Will Brown."

Pearl reached out her hand to Will, "Howdy!"

Will politely shook her hand, sat down at the table and Kohler ordered drinks. "Draw me a beer and give Will a Coke."

Kohler watched Will's face as he looked over the room of cowboys and cowgirls. He observed him grinning as he read the signs around the room.

NEVER APPROACH A BULL FROM THE FRONT, A HORSE FROM THE REAR, OR A FOOL FROM ANY DIRECTION.

COURAGE IS BEING SCARED TO DEATH AND SADDLING UP ANYWAY.

Over a picture of John Wayne a sign read: TALK LOW, TALK SLOW AND DON'T SAY TOO MUCH.

One near the restroom said: DON'T SQUAT WITH YOUR SPURS ON.

And a sign over the cash register said: CASH, ASS OR GRASS – NO CREDIT.

Pearl brought a draft beer in a mug for Kohler and a Coke in a big Coca-Cola glass for Will. Kohler swallowed the foamy, cold beer and asked Will, "What are you thinking?"

Will sipped on the Coke and sighed. "I'm thinkin' I've never been in a place like this."

Suddenly, there was a disturbance on the dance floor and a fight broke out. The Blue Goose bouncer, a huge woman named Hannah, grabbed both young combatants by the collar and physically threw them out the front door. The room filled with laughter and Hannah smugly slapped her hands together like she'd just finished a cleaning project.

Kohler explained, "Hannah's a dangerous woman. The Marines could use her. Someone wrote a western song about her called 'Hard Hearted Hannah, The Vamp From Savannah."

The jukebox was only a few feet away from their table and reminded Will of the jukebox at Ruth's Café back home. Someone had dropped coins in the machine and pushed the plastic buttons for their selection. Will saw the record dropped in place and a romantic song began, inspiring couples to slow dance. He thought about Laverne. He didn't think she'd want him to be in a bar.

Meanwhile, Taggart, a burly man with a broken nose, whose appearance reminded Will of the story of Paul Bunyan, strode to the back of the room where Kohler and Will were seated. Two men were following him and all three men were glaring at Kohler. They stopped at the table and Taggart spoke.

"They tell me you think you're the bare knuckled champ of this county."

Will noticed that Kohler seemed to be ignoring Taggart. There was a rustling of chairs in the tables near them as individuals moved out of the way. This was followed by a quiet which made it easy to hear Pearl calling, "Hannah!"

Taggart continued, "I don't like for someone to challenge the title which is rightfully mine."

Will felt frozen to his seat and was confounded to see Kohler smiling at him. Finally, Kohler turned his head to look at Taggart and said, slowly emphasizing each word, "Did anyone ever tell you you're one...ugly...son of a bitch?"

Taggart frowned, his eyes watered and his big nose turned red. Then he reached out his hand to grab the remainder of Kohler's beer to throw it in his face, but Kohler's response was swift. With all his strength, he seized Taggart's hand in a tight deadlock before he could move the glass mug. Through clenched teeth Kohler asked, "Do you want to dance here or outside?"

Before Taggart answered, Hannah appeared with a club in her hand ready to swing. "Think seriously about how you want to answer that question Taggart."

Kohler and Taggart voluntarily proceeded outdoors to the boxing ring while Will was roughly, involuntarily moved by Taggart's two cohorts.

Taggart, who was behind Kohler when they entered the ring, managed to throw the first temporarily debilitating punch. While Kohler was still down, he saw Will pummeled by Taggart's mean friends in the parking lot. He yelled at him in the DI voice which Will was accustomed to obeying. "Start throwing punches Brown! When Marines come in second, they die." Then Kohler kicked Taggart between the legs, quickly ending the fight with him.

Meanwhile, obeying orders, Will at last began punching his opponents with all his might. Surprised at his own muscular strength, he knocked them out, one at a time to the applause of appreciative unlookers. Kohler continued to applaud Will as everyone drifted back to the bar. "Brown, welcome to my world."

Both nursed their injuries from the fight as they headed back to the base, stopping two miles out so Will could change clothes and get in the trunk until the coast was clear and he could return to his quarters without notice.

The following day the recruits were given pugil sticks for practicing aggression to the enemy once again. Will faced recruit Johnson who had previously repeatedly harassed him because he seemed timid. When the whistle blew, Will immediately attacked Johnson, knocking him down and hitting him.

Sergeant Jakobowski had to blow his whistle several times to stop the combat and asked, "What the hell did Brown have for breakfast? What has happened to our humble soul?"

Just as Kohler had hoped, Will's experience in the Blue Goose parking lot helped Will to grow in confidence. But nothing more would ever be said about the incident. It was nobody's business and Will could be trusted with the sergeant's secret entertainment outlet.

Most of the recruits considered Kohler to be just another callous DI, but Will had seen him in another light. The man had his respect, and despite what everyone else thought, he knew Kohler had a big heart and endeavored to make strong men out of each individual in his platoon. Although his methods were awfully rough, he was successful in teaching the recruits to be Marines.

However, some were slow learners, and Pete Springer seemed to be in that category. Will was acquainted with Pete's undisciplined background. He had grown up without much parenting and was left on his own most of the time. But Pete had always been his faithful friend, and he knew Pete would eventually learn to follow the rules too.

One day Will noticed Pete was sitting on his bunk, carefully cutting off the collar and part of the shoulder from his shirt. Will socked him, "What are you doing? You just ruined a good shirt."

Pete kept cutting. "I know, but standing out there in a wool uniform in ninety degree heat aint exactly fun. Besides, nobody will ever know I just have a collar for a shirt. My jacket will cover my chest."

Will shook his head.

On inspection day, Kohler ordered the platoon to prepare for inspection. He commanded, "Open ranks harch." As usual, Kohler's pronunciation for "march" always sounded like "harch."

Nevertheless, the first squad took two steps forward and the second squad took one step forward. Then Kohler saluted the Inspecting Officer. "Platoon 101 prepared for inspection, Sir."

The stern faced Inspecting Officer asked Kohler to precede him. As they moved through the platoon, the Inspecting Officer commented, "They look sharp Sergeant Kohler. Now have the men remove their jackets to make sure their belt lengths are two to four inches."

Kohler ordered, "Remove your jackets."

All the recruits obeyed except for Pete Springer who stood very still and hoped he'd be invisible. But it wasn't working. Kohler stormily commanded him. "Remove your jacket, Springer!"

Pete slowly removed his jacket. The shoulders of the other recruits shook as they tried to keep from laughing out loud. Seeing Pete's bare white skin glowing in the sun, Kohler looked up at the sky and rolled his eyes.

The Inspecting Officer gave Kohler an insulting smile and left. Kohler saluted him and turned furiously to Pete. "Springer! Give me fifty pushups. Now! Do you realize you've destroyed government property?"

In the afternoon, the recruits wore green t-shirts, khaki shorts and tennis shoes as they did calisthenics. Even though they were dressed cooler, the sweat poured off them as they did strenuous exercises including squat thrust, pushups, side straddle hops, running in place and toe touches.

Kohler proudly watched his platoon from a window of his office while he was catching up on paperwork. Drill Instructor, Locker Box Jones tapped on the office door and Kohler invited him in. There was a portrait of General Chesty Puller on the wall behind the desk and Jones commented on it.

"What a legend. They should have made a movie out of his life. I heard the only medal that Puller didn't have was the Medal of Honor."

Kohler nodded his head. "Yep, you're right. There's scuttlebutt that he tried to trade five Navy Crosses for it."

Jones laughed heartily. Then he curiously studied the unfinished project Kohler had going at a table in the corner. There was a bottle of olive drab paint, a paint brush and a couple blue practice grenades. "What do you have going on here?"

Kohler walked over to the table and explained. "101 is going to the rifle range next week and they'll be throwing hand grenades. I'm going to paint a blue practice grenade olive drab, the same color as a live fragmentation grenade. During my instruction, I'll act like I'm accidentally dropping a live grenade with the pin out. Then I'll see if I have a hero that would throw his body over it to save his fellow marines."

Jones shook his head. "I hope it don't backfire on you."

14

Marksmanship Training

Early one sunny morning, Platoon 101 was transported in buses to the area designated as the rifle range to begin two weeks of training. Will Brown and Pete Springer had both been enthusiastic about this activity. They were familiar with using rifles through their hunting experiences in West Virginia and were anxious to fire their new weapons.

Pete was goofy with anticipation and punched Will as they got off the bus. "Oh boy, this looks like home on the range. Get it? Home on the range."

Will didn't pay any attention to him but recruit Ruiz who moved off the bus behind them, laughed at him, satisfying Pete's perpetual need to entertain. The cheerful Mexican slapped Pete's back and said, "You're loco, Springer! You keep me grinning."

The recruits were first ushered into the Rifle Range Classroom where they were told what they could expect through marksmanship training. The tall, smiling, good-natured instructor elaborated.

"Rifle competition is very significant to the Marines. It's as popular to the Marines as football is to Texas. Every year, matches are held across the country including those at Camp Lejeune, Camp Pendleton and Hawaii. This is followed by the Marine Corps Championship at Camp Lejeune and the Inner Service Match at Quantico, Virginia. Shooters from across the states, including civilians, ultimately compete at Camp Perry Ohio for the National Rifle and Pistol Championship. From this level shooters are selected for the Olympics and snipers are chosen. Do your best and make the Marines proud of you."

A second instructor without smiles was introduced to the class. He gave instructions without enthusiasm as if they had been memorized and repeated often. "You will be firing from 200, 300 and 500 yards while you are in four positions including sitting, kneeling, offhand and prone. There will be smudge pots at the range. Invest in amber glasses, remember to blacken your sights and use a sticky substance on your shoulder. You will be expected to keep good records. Be aware that many things affect your shooting accuracy. Wind, temperature, air density, sight picture, position and trigger squeeze are some of the things of which you need to be continually aware. For instance, one click of windage will move you one inch for every hundred yards. In a little while you will go outside, and in single file form a circle around the 55 gallon drum that's painted white in the center with black dots. This will give you the same sight picture as on the firing range. For three days, you will practice using the four positions for firing. You will adjust slings and snap in. Eventually, one DI will be assigned to every four shooters. Half of this platoon will fire each morning while the other half pulls targets in the butts, then alternating in the afternoon. Only Coaches will clear jammed weapons or misfires. Weapons will always be pointed down range. And when you are moving from 200 to 300 yards, and 300 to 500 yards, the weapons will be in sling arms. The non-commissioned officer will control every move with a bullhorn from the tower which is centered in the middle of the range. Listen to the Range Master and good luck on the range."

The amplified voice of the Tower NCO boomed out across the 200 yard line. "First relay, move up on the firing line. Get yourself in a good sitting position and make sure you fire on your own target. Second relay, move up to the ready box. All shooters should have their slings on their arms. First stage of fire will be five rounds slow fire in the sitting position at 200 yards. On the firing line with five rounds, lock and load. Are you ready on the right? Are you ready on the left?"

The coaches signaled that they were ready by raising their hands.

The Tower NCO continued, "All ready on the firing line. Commence firing when your target appears."

The hearts of the recruits, especially those who never fired a weapon, were beating at a faster pace at the command, and adrenalin kept all of them alert as they watched for their target.

The pit NCO who was in direct communication with the Tower, waited three seconds before he ordered all the targets raised. Then for several more seconds, the sound of rifle fire resounded up and down the firing line until the time limit expired and the NCO yelled. "Cease fire! Cease fire! Unload and lock your weapons. Coaches, check all weapons. Is the line clear? Clear on the right? Clear on the left?"

The coaches signaled that the line was clear. Then the Tower NCO repeated the sequence of commands for the offhand position. After each relay, everyone moved back to the 300 yard line in the sitting positions for rapid fire and ending at the 500 yard line prone position for slow fire.

Eventually, when the tower NCO announced the final "Cease fire," all ammunition was secured and the line cleared, and the pit detail could emerge from the butts for the mid-day break.

Twenty year old, disgruntled Steve Hossman was a proud coon hunter from Harlan County Kentucky. He didn't like the feel of the Marine rifle and blaimed his target misses on the weapon. Finally, the coach addressed him. "Hossman, you've fired three Maggie's drawers in a row. What's the problem?" Hossman complained, "It ain't my fault. It's this goldarn rifle."

The coach took the rifle and after carefully examining it, handed it back. "The problem is not your rifle or the dope on the rifle. The problem is the dope behind the rifle."

Hossman had bragged about his shooting skill to the other recruits and now they were looking at him.

His face turned bright red and he stammered, "This dang rifle fires poorly."

The coach asked, "So, back in Kentucky, how would you correct your rifle if it was firing to the left or to the right?"

Hossman scratched his head. "Why, I'd stick the barrel between two stumps and just bend the barrel a little."

With wrinkled brow, the coach moved directly in front of Hossman, spraying Hossman's face with each forceful word out of his mouth. "Well Hossman, there's your way, my way and the Marine Corps way. Guess who's way we're going to follow?"

Hossman wiped his face with his sleeve. "The Marine Corps way, Sir."

Pistol range day was another challenge for the recruits. Will Brown and Pete Springer had never fired pistols, but they were looking forward to firing them. They soon learned that rifle and pistol safety procedures and sequences were similar. They were told to shoot at the silhouette, black head and shoulder targets that the Range Master turned with a lever.

On the 15 yard line bench, there was a large bucket of green paint from which workers had been painting benches and podiums earlier that day. It was Pete Springer's turn to fire from 25 yards, but when he fired the pistol, he exploded the bucket of paint and the 15 yard line bench was blown to pieces.

The pistol range NCO had already had a bad day trying to get a couple of know-it-alls to follow procedures. He screamed at Springer, "I've got civilians to mow my lawn and keep it green and I don't need you to mow my grass with a 45 pistol!"

When the NCO settled down, he attempted to correct Springer. "You're jerking the trigger. When you jerk the trigger, you either buck it high or pull it low. The secret to shooting is to squeeeeeze the trigger with a constant pressure so that when the weapon fires, it is a complete surprise to you. It's like squeezing a woman's breast until you get your gun off."

Springer smiled so big that he showed a missing molar from his top teeth that normally wasn't noticed. The NCO continued. "Pick up your pistol and load your five round magazine. Now aim in and get a good sight picture and start squeezing...slowly, slowly, slowly." The pistol fired.

"Now put your pistol down. Did you know it was going to fire?"

Pete quickly put his pistol down. "Sir, no. It surprised me, Sir."

To Pete's delight, the range NCO checked the target and found that he had hit it dead center.

Sergeant Kohler met with Platoon 101 in one of the empty Quonset huts for teaching the recruits what they needed to know about hand grenades. He had already shown them how to differentiate from a blue practice grenade and a real grenade.

"Tomorrow you will be throwing live hand grenades." At his announcement, there wasn't a sound in the room, but one could feel imperceptible gasps from the inexperienced recruits. Stories had been passed around the base about how a careless recruit had recently lost a foot. They didn't know that the bogus story initiated from one of the DI's, merely as a scare tactic so that the recruits would be cautious. They all listened to Kohler attentively.

"You will be in a bunker with an instructor." Kohler looked into the eyes of one individual who appeared fearful. "Remember, as long as you hold the lever down, nothing happens. However, if you pull the pin and the lever is released, the grenade will explode in five seconds."

"First, the instructor will command you to pull the pin—at which time you will pull the pin making sure the lever is down. The second command will be to prepare to throw—at which time you will take a stance with your throwing arm back. The next command will be to throw the grenade—at which time you will lob the grenade and crouch down in the sand-bagged bunker."

As Kohler spoke to the class, he put his right hand inside his pocket and handled the practice grenade which he had carefully painted the color of a real grenade.

"In actual combat or training, if a live grenade falls in the midst of you and your fellow Marines, the one nearest the grenade will throw his helmet and his body over the grenade, saving the lives of his fellow marines." Taking the phoney grenade from his pocket, Kohler held it up, pulled the pin and replaced the pin while holding the lever down.

Certain that all the recruits are watching, he held up the grenade a second time and pulled the pin. Then he pretended he was replacing the pin while accidentally dropping the grenade. With a theatrical fearful look on his face, Kohler yelled, "Fire in the hole!

The classroom exploded, not by the grenade, but rather by the stampede of recruits. Several men made an instant beeline to the windows and dived out, but most of the men rushed to the only door. In their haste, they pushed each other towards the exit, and in the panic and chaos, Kohler and another man were accidentally knocked down.

The terrified young man who was knocked down with Kohler was frozen with fear as he saw the grenade just inches from his feet. When the practice grenade popped like a dud firecracker followed by a small trickle of smoke, the recruit fainted.

That night, sitting on their bunks in the Quonset hut, the recruits laughed about the incidents of the day. Pete Springer effectively mimicked Sergeant Kohler's words and expressions, bringing the weary men to tearful fits of laughter. He'd mastered Kohler's pronunciations and tones. After he entertained his buddies for a while, exhaustion finally had it's way and he hollered, "Platoon 101, on the double, harch! Get your asses into your bunk and sleep!"

A recruit in a bunk near Pete's commented in a low, sleepy voice, "Napolean Bonaparte said, 'The first virtue in a soldier is endurance of fatigue; courage is only the second virtue.'"

Sergeant Kohler wore a shoulder sling for a few days because his supposed harmless prank backfired. On Rifle Qualification Day, he stood on the sidelines. It was gratifying to him to see Platoon 101 make an incredible showing. Eight of his men had made Expert, fifteen had made Sharpshooter and twenty-eight qualified as Marksmen.

Will Brown and Pete Springer had both been awarded Sharpshooter. As the Series Commander presented the platoon with the Marksmanship trophy, their gleaming sunburned faces, streaked with gun powder and oil, were full of smiles. Will glanced at Kohler and noticed he was also smiling. The sergeant, gave him a quick, inconspicuous thumbs up when he looked his way.

The recruits had faced the ceaseless grinds of training. So when Sergeant Jakobowski told them their next experience would be a full week of Mess Duty, they thought it might be easy. They dreamed of gorging themselves with steak, pie and ice cream while they worked in the Marine kitchen.

They were awakened from their dreams at 0300, and after they showered and shaved and hastened to line up outside in three ranks, they marched to the Second Battalion Mess Hall. There, the Mess Sergeant began teaching them the preliminary work that must be done to feed a company of men.

The recruits changed into white trousers, white t-shirts, white caps, white rubber gloves and everyone was given an assignment. They learned to work together as never before. Some were given specific positions in the steam line, scullery or pot shack. Others were assigned to the salad room or the store room. Some had the responsibility of preparing juice or coffee. There was much to be done, and despite the good smells of things like bacon, baked bread or other dishes emanating from the kitchen, they soon learned that taste testing wasn't allowed.

Pete Springer and recruit Ruiz spent the morning peeling hundreds of potatoes. To kill the time, the two men had been having a discussion about the food they missed from home. Pete had admitted he sorely missed his sardines, and also the special chili cheese dogs at Ruth's Café. Pete noticed Ruiz had a tear in his eye when he shared the fact that he really missed his mother's homemade tortillas, but Pete could see it was probably his mother that Ruiz missed the most.

That same morning, Will Brown was assigned to an area with a huge, flat grill where pancakes would be prepared for breakfast. He and a tall recruit, nicknamed Stretch, poured out creamy batter in rounds with a diameter of about four inches on the hot grill. At a certain point when the dough began to bubble, they used metal pancake turners to flip them. After Will got the hang of it, it became monotonous work, and as he stood there he began to think about Laverne. There was still almost two weeks left at boot camp. And he wasn't the only recruit feeling homesick.

15

Waiting For News

Laverne Alderman was always anxious to get home from her job at the Raleigh County Recorder's office so she could see if she received a letter from Will. When she opened the mailbox, she gave a delighted squeal as she saw his handwriting on the envelope. She held the envelope to her lips and ran up to the porch swing when she sat down to read the letter.

Meanwhile, her mother, Nina Alderman, who had been visiting with a neighbor, walked back to the house, observing her daughter's glow as she approached the porch. "I see you received a letter from Will."

Laverne held up the letter. "He's graduating in ten days—and he wants me to come to the ceremony."

On the same afternoon, Radar barked at the mailman with a single woof, signaling the Brown family that the mail had arrived. Little Becky and Milford raced to the homemade, wooden mailbox beside the road, with Milford arriving first to find Will's letter. Holding it over his head so that his sister couldn't reach it, he teased her. Little Becky defiantly swung around and ran back to the house bawling, "It's a letter from Will and Milford won't let me see it." Tears splashed from her eyes until finally, Milford ran after her to stop her so he wouldn't be in trouble for making her cry.

"Here, Little Becky. You can hold it."

The whimpering ceased, but her bottom lip was thrust out as she wiped the tears from her eyes with her sleeve. "I just wanted to see if Will got my medal for show and tell."

Milford corrected her, "Well you can't see. It's addressed to Dad."

Inside the house, the family sat together at the table, impatiently waiting while Walter Brown read the letter. Velma asked, "Well...what does he have to say?"

Walter handed the letter to his wife and got up from the table, pulled a large handkerchief from his pocket and blew his nose.

Milford and Little Becky watched their mother as they waited to hear about their big brother. Velma's love and motherly pride for her son showed on her face and in her voice as she finally spoke.

"My, my. This is quite a change from his earlier letters. He says it hasn't been easy, but he finally understands what they're tryin' to do. He says he has learned a lot and is being prepared for manhood. The tough sergeant he hated, is now someone he respects. And he wants us to meet him when we come to his graduation ceremony."

Walter, contemplatively, slowly sat down at the table again and Little Becky, eyes wide jumped out of her chair and lifted her arms so Walter would pick her up and let her sit in his lap. When he did, she put her arms around his neck and asked, "Can we go, Daddy? Pleeeeze?"

Milford anxiously watched his father's face to see how he would respond, well-acquainted with his expressions, both positive and negative. Then when he knew what Walter's face was saying, he hollered, "Yahoo! We get to go to a Marine graduation."

Hearing the excitement, Radar stood outside at the back door waiting to be invited inside.

16

More To Learn

All of Platoon 101 just happened to be lined up outdoors when the Officer of the Day arrived on the base. The platoon had just received orders to present themselves in an unusually awkward and humbling position. Their ungracious pose was necessarily brought about because several cases of the notorious "crabs" were discovered by the Medic and needed to be eradicated from the base. Every one of the recruits had been ordered to remove their pants and bend over as if they were mooning someone, showing their bare butts.

The Officer of the Day was not aware of the situation and was obviously mortified by the display. As He approached the Mess Sergeant who was giving the orders, he bellowed, "Sergeant, what inferno exhibition is going on here? Is this the way you show respect to a Senior Officer?"

The Mess Sergeant, who was feeling very uncomfortable with the situation, bluntly explained. "The men on mess duty caught the crabs and we're going to be...well...we're going to be spraying assholes. They aren't mooning you, Sir."

Meanwhile, a Marine jeep arrived with a spray rig trailer, and it was driven down the line of bare butts, spraying each with a guaranteed, crab killing, blistering chemical that immediately caused the recruits to run for the showers.

The officer, finally seeing the reason for the peculiar spectacle, raised both of his hands, shook his head and walked away saying, "Leave it to the Marines! Well, I guess that's one way to get the job done."

The Mess Sergeant gave a mission accomplished sigh and strode back to the kitchen.

The recruits spent many hours in the classroom in the next few days beginning with a class concerning squad tactics. The instructor explained many details.

"A Marine rifle squad consists of three four-man teams and a squad leader. Each fire team has one man that carries a Browning Automatic Rifle. In most scenarios, a squad leader can communicate with his fire teams by hand and arm signals. Depending on the situation, he may have two fire teams lay down a field of fire and use the third fire team to attack the enemy's flank.

The Marine squad leader is like a football quarterback. He may have one fire team lay down a field of fire and attack the enemy on both flanks with the remaining fire teams.

There are also platoon tactics, company tactics, battalion tactics and regimental tactics. That's why when units lose men, they regroup into an organized fighting unit. This happened on Tarawa when bad tide intelligence placed the attacking force in the water, hundreds of yards from their beachhead. Even though hundreds were killed in the water, they regrouped and took the island."

Later, the recruits were instructed on the "field transport pack." The pack included a blanket rolled inside a ½ tent and poncho, mess gear, three days rations, ammo, extra boots, three sets of underwear and socks, and a small shovel or entrenching tool.

After the recruits were familiar with the field transport pack, they attended a class which taught them to use a compass, maps, find directions by the stars and tell the time merely by looking at shadows. They learned how to align a map with a compass and how to make overlays, even on toilet paper.

Before they moved outdoors again, the recruits were familiarized with the "Five Paragraph Combat Order." It included Information, Mission, Administration, Support Arms and Communication.

Part of the training included going into a simulated war zone. Here they experienced machine gun fire, artillery explosions, barbwire and smoke. It was the nearest they could be to a real battlefield with combat action and still be safe.

This simulated environment felt profoundly like a real war zone, and many individuals found that they lost concentration on the techniques they had been taught in fire team tactics. Bombarded and distracted by noises, smells and other psychological disturbances, it wasn't easy to keep one's mind on the objective. Nevertheless, it served a great purpose, convincing the men of the need to practice and perfect the art of war through further discipline and preparation in the fleet Marine force. They became more determined than ever to learn how to conquer enemy strongholds.

The recruits absorbed more information than they ever dreamed possible in the following days. And in between their instruction time, Sergeant Kohler ran the platoon three miles with no stragglers.

Graduation day was soon approaching and they were grateful to at last be given some "time off" for studying for their final exam and to prepare for their final inspection.

When final Inspection Day arrived, the inspection team was top heavy with brass. Two Captains preceded by two lieutenants meticulously checked everything on each recruit, from clean fingernails to shaved faces. There were audible sighs of relief when the platoon finally passed inspection.

The next hurdle for the recruits was Exam Day. Sergeant Kohler could feel the tension of the platoon as they entered the classroom for the exam. But that evening, as he reviewed the test answers, he was pleased with the results. They were ready for graduation.

17

Graduation

The recruits were in their quarters preparing for the ceremonies that would soon take place outdoors. Will Brown read Laverne's letter again one last time. The letter informed him that she would be coming to his graduation along with his parents. She would probably be on the base with his family by now.

Pete Springer stood in front of Will, distracting him from his thoughts. Pete flexed his muscles and bragged, "I'm a fightin' machine, Will. Do I look good or what?"

Will rolled his eyes. "Yeah, Pete. You'll be a real lady killer back home, as long as you don't get sardine breath again."

Pete ignored him and continued, "I'm a new man. Eleven weeks, and I'm a new man. And look at you too, Will." Will knew Pete was referring to his physique, but Will was considering the changes in him that weren't so obvious. For the first time in his life, he felt confident as he looked forward to the future. As he contemplated his plans, the recruits were called to attention and Sergeant Kohler entered the room with an announcement.

"We came in second for Honor Platoon!" The recruits shouted and clapped. Kohler continued. "One man in Platoon 101 was chosen as Honor Recruit and will receive a set of blues. This award is given to the recruit who is the most improved and who also has shown ability to work harmoniously with others. I am pleased to announce that a unanimous decision was made by your superiors to choose Will Brown as Honor Recruit."

The platoon applauded the decision and some of the men shook Will's hand. Pete Springer slapped his back and grinned at Will who appeared to be amazed.

"Can you beat that? My friend, Will Brown is the Honor Recruit. Is this the same person as the 4th grader who hid in the boy's restroom when little Penelope Lane threatened to sock him in the nose if he didn't give her his peanut butter sandwich?"

The bleachers were full of the recruit's family members and friends.

Among the crowd, Laverne sat beside the Brown Family, attentively watching for Will. They were all aware that Will and his friend, Pete Springer had both made Private First Class. Will had been assigned an MOS of 3500 motor transport. Pete had been assigned an MOS of 0300 grunt. Both of them would be stationed at Camp Lejeune, North Carolina.

Little Becky jumped up and pointed Will out to everybody as soon as he appeared with his platoon. "There he is! That's my brother!"

When Milford spotted him, his eyes widened as he stared. "Wow, look at him! He looks so cool. Man oh man! I hope some day I'll wear a uniform like that."

The pride that Milford felt was felt by all his family. Both his mother and Laverne had tears sparkling in their eyes. Walter took off his glasses and polished them with the front of his shirt. The band was playing the poignant Marine Hymn and as they watched the impressive ceremonial parade, they noticed many people in the bleachers were moved at seeing their sons and brothers and friends in uniform.

The recruits were formed into perfectly lined-up platoons in front of the Adjutant and Commanding Officers who were facing the troops. The First Platoon Leader reported, "First Platoon all accounted for, Sir." He saluted the Adjutant and the Adjutant returned the salute. Then Platoon's two, three and four reported and followed suit.

The Adjutant did an about face and reported to the Commanding Officer. "All present and accounted for, Sir."

The Commanding Officer responded, "Post the orders."

The Adjutant did an about face and faced the troops. "Attention to orders, Officer of the Day, Lieutenant Jones, Officers center march."

On the commands, Platoon Leaders and Guidon Bearers of the First and Second Platoons did a left face. Platoon leaders and Guidon Bearers of the Third and Fourth Platoons did a right face. Guidon Bearers were carrying small red flags with the platoon number.

Platoon leaders and Guidon Bearers marched to the center of the platoons facing each other. Then they faced and marched to the Adjutant, stopped and saluted. Guidon Bearers lowered their guidons in salute and then returned them upright. Platton leaders and Guidon bearers did an about face and returned to their platoons. The Adjutant did an about face and reported to the Commanding Officer, "Sir, the orders are posted."

After the Commanding Officer ordered, "Pass in review," the Adjutant did an about face to the Platoon Leaders and commanded, "Pass in review."

The orders were given: "Right face," and Platoon Leaders and Guidon Bearers took position in front of the platoons. Then with "Forward March," the Marine Base Band stepped off drums and the platoons picked up the beat as the band played Semper Fidelis.

The Marine Hymn was played as the platoons passed in review before the Commanding Officer. The Platoon Leaders commanded "Eyes right," and when they passed, "Eyes front."

The entire Marine graduation ceremony was, and is, and will always be, a deeply momentous experience, known only to Marines who have experienced the proud team spirit called Esprit De Corps.

After the ceremony and the parade were over, the Marines joined their families and loved ones. There was much embracing and handshaking, tears of joy and marathon kisses, with Laverne and Will as high competitors for the record length of a kiss.

Sergeant Kohler and his young son, Victor, who was dressed in his little green uniform as usual, asked to be introduced to Will's family and Laverne. Kohler shook hands with Walter and Velma while Victor politely held his hand out so he could shake hands with Milford and Little Becky.

Little Becky took one look at the miniature "Marine" and boldly stated in amazement, "You're too little to be a Marine. How come you didn't grow?"

Everyone laughed except Victor who stamped his foot and quickly returned, "My dad is the sergeant," as if that explained everything.

Kohler gave his best smile to Laverne. "So you're the young lady I've heard so much about." Then with a sideways glance at Will, Kohler asked her, "Would you like me to take you on a tour of the base...alone?"

Will knew Kohler was flirting and quickly responded, putting his arm tightly around Laverne. "Oh no you don't!" And everyone laughed some more.

Meanwhile, Pete Springer appeared with his mother, and more introductions were made. Mrs. Springer already knew the Browns because they lived in the same community for years. When Will and Pete went back to their quarters to get their things to take home, the two mothers talked about the obvious changes in their sons. And when Walter and Velma Brown eventually had a moment alone with Sergeant Kohler, they thanked him for helping Will to grow in confidence.

18

Back Home

It was late at night when Walter pulled the car up to Laverne's house to drop her off. She had fallen asleep on Will's shoulder in the back seat with Little Becky asleep on her lap. After scooting over so Laverne could lay Little Becky on the seat, Will got out and held the car door open for Laverne as she slid out of the car and whispered "Thanks for taking me" to Walter and then "Good night everyone." Will kissed her goodnight and waved at Nina Alderman who had come out of the house and stood waiting for her daughter under the light at the front door.

When the Brown's arrived home, Will looked for Radar to come down the driveway, but somehow, the dog had been left inside the house. He could be seen looking out the window with his tail wagging madly. When the door to the house was opened, Radar flew into Will, and standing on his hind feet with his front paws on Wills chest and tongue slapping his face, he welcomed him home.

Walter carried Little Becky to her bed and Milford went immediately to his. Everyone was exhausted from the memorable day, but the three adults sat down at the kitchen table to talk anyway. Velma brought out a plate of Will's favorite homemade cookies and handed him a cold glass of milk. She was the first to speak as she moved behind his chair and kissed his head. "We've missed you. How does it feel to be home, son?"

Will devoured a cookie before he spoke. "Thanks Mom. It's good to be home. That was the longest eleven weeks of my life. But it was worth it all."

Walter asked him, "Was it as tough as everybody says it is?"

"Tough enough. But the stress is gone now and I'll enjoy some peace and quiet. Well, at least until I see Frankie Ragsdale."

Velma gave a worried glance to Walter whereupon he merely cautioned her with his look—which meant she should not say anything yet.

The three Browns sat at the table and talked for hours. Will wanted to know everything that had been happening on the farm, Walter wanted to hear more details about Parris Island, and Velma wanted to know more about Will's plans for the future.

Will shared, "I haven't told Laverne yet, because I wanted to discuss it with her when we can be alone. But Jimmy T wrote me and said he really wants to pay for the wedding when we figure out the date. After we're married, I'll put in for base housing. I discovered, because of the war in Vietnam, there's no waiting list."

Later that night, after the cookies and milk had disappeared, Velma excused herself and went to bed, but Will and his dad remained at the table. Walter was impressed with the maturity he saw in Will, and Will was enjoying the unusual interest that his dad was showing. He told Walter about the Blue Goose trip with Sergeant Kohler. When he had finished telling the experience and how it had affected him, Walter said, "It sounds like that trip was illegal."

Will nodded. "Sergeant Kohler says 'Sometimes you have to break the rules to get the job done.'"

The next morning when the rooster crowed, Will jumped out of bed thinking he'd missed reveille. But seeing he wasn't in a Quonset Hut, he fell back on his bed in relief. He pulled the quilt back over his head and tried to go back to sleep, but it was useless. After habitually getting up before dawn for so many weeks, he wasn't able to settle back down and he was wide awake.

Will decided to get dressed and run a mile or two. An enthusiastic Radar seemed ready to go with him. But lazy Radar stopped and turned back after only following Will's brisk pace down the driveway to the road.

After a couple miles of running, Will saw Pete coming down the road from the other direction. When they met, Will asked him, "What are you doing running out here this early in the morning?"

"I was about to ask you the same thing...but I already know the answer. We got too used to getting up early, huh?"

They laughed, and then Will invited Pete to run back home with him for "a cup of Joe."

By the time they got back to the farm, Velma was fixing breakfast and Walter sat at the table drinking his coffee. Will's friend Charlie Shipman, who had become Walter's handyman since Will joined the Marines, pulled into the driveway in Will's old pickup truck, reminding Will he needed to figure out his transportation for going into town.

Before Will and Pete went into the house, they greeted Charlie who commented on their builds. "My, my. You boys got in shape! They're lookin' for a new security man over at the Raleigh County Recorder's office. You two might be able to handle it." He teased, "Of course it would take the two of you to replace one of me."

Standing on each side of Charlie, Will and Pete punched him hard at the same time, making Charlie chuckle, "Don't tickle me."

Will asked, "I guess you like working here on the farm better than at the Recorder's Office? Dad said you're a great help."

"Yeah. I figure I'll stay on unless you try to take back my job from me now that you have a little muscle."

"Naw. I think I'll stick with the Marines. They're easier on me than Dad is."

The night before, Will had offered to help Walter on the farm but Walter had surprisingly insisted that he wanted Will to have some time off.

Velma stuck her head out the back door of the house and yelled, "Hey you boys, come on in before your breakfast gets cold. You too, Charlie."

Velma had prepared buckwheat pancakes. Milford was already putting butter and an enormous amount of maple syrup on a stack of three. Walter reprimanded Milford while taking the syrup pitcher from him. "Milford! You don't need to float a battleship." Then turning to Little Becky who was elaborately decorating her pancake with blueberries, Walter advised, "Pick up your fork and eat your breakfast!"

When the threesome walked into the house, Velma invited Pete and Charlie to sit down at the table. But Will took the pancake turner and the batter pitcher from his mother after she had taken the pancakes off the grill. Then he poured out the creamy batter in rounds with a diameter of about four inches and waited for them to form little bubbles before he flipped them.

Velma was tickled by his actions and told him, "Well, I guess the Marines did teach you...something."

Pete, who shoveled another fork filled with pancake into his mouth as if he was starving, paused for a moment. "The Marines didn't make 'em taste like this!"

Walter was done eating so he moved out to the porch to put on his boots, signaling Charlie that he better eat quick, which he did. After politely thanking "Mrs. Brown," Charlie followed Walter out the door. Then, appearing to forget something, Charlie turned around, reached in his pocket, pulled out his keys, and threw them at Will. "You can use my wheels today if you want."

Later, that morning, after he gave Pete a ride back home, Will drove past the billboard at the side of the highway that had inspired him to enlist in the Marines.

THE MARINE CORPS BUILDS MEN BODY, SOUL AND SPIRIT.

"Yep!" He said out loud and grinned at himself in the rear view mirror. Then although he hadn't prayed much, something made him add in reverent sincerity, "Thank God."

Back at the farm, Will went out to the barn to check on the animals. Milford had done a good job. The cages were clean and the animals all looked healthy and well fed. The rabbit population seemed to have multiplied and Milford had found a turtle somewhere.

As Will examined the turtle, which pulled his snake-like head into his hard shell when he turned him over, Milford appeared. "Pretty cool turtle huh Will?"

"Yeah. He's neat. And you've done a good job with the animals, Milford."

"Thanks. I guess it'll always be my job now that you plan' to get hitched and move to North Carolina. But that's okay. I like the animals." Milford paused and stared at his big brother a moment before continuing. "But I'll miss you, Will."

The two looked at each other fondly. Then Milford changed the subject and laughed. "At least I'll get my room back to myself."

Laverne Alderman worked eight hours a day, five days a week at the Raleigh County Recorder's office. She liked her job and she was a valuable employee, but with Will back home, it was hard for her to keep her mind on her work.

They saw each other every evening after work. They often ate dinner together with Will's family at the farm. Other times, Laverne's mother, Nina Alderman or even Laverne herself proved their excellent cooking skills and prepared dinner. Some nights, Will and Laverne met in the back corner of Ruth's café. On one romantic night together, they decided that December 1st would be a good wedding date.

Laverne had begun making plans for the day she had dreamed about since she was a child. She asked her cousin, Cheryl, to be her Maid of Honor,

Little Becky would be her flower girl, and her bridesmaids were longtime friends from high school.

Will's older brother, Jimmy T, who seemed to be rolling in dough from his dry cleaning business in Charleston, had generously insisted on paying for the wedding. He even personally gave Laverne a blank check for her to purchase the material for her bride's dress and her attendant's dresses.

19

Payback

A couple of weeks before December, Will and Laverne, Pete Springer and his new girlfriend, Latoya, went on a double-date and attended a Saturday night dance at the Legion Hall. Both men looked handsome in their dress green Marine uniforms. Laverne wore a pleated skirt with a cream-colored sweater and Latoya wore a corduroy jumper with a polka-dotted blouse.

As usual, the Legion Hall building was full of loud music and laughter. The two couples sat at the table near the back wall where Will and Laverne had sat on the night that Will was humiliated by Frankie Ragsdale.

Pete spotted his former girlfriend, Linda sitting by herself. He'd heard that her engagement to Billy Hedrick was broken off and she was single again. She was looking forlornly at Pete, and Latoya noticed. Pete took Latoya's hand. "Don't worry 'bout her. She's history. I want a girl I can trust. Let's dance!" Latoya blushed and Pete winked at her as they moved to the dance floor.

Laverne asked Will, "Did the Marines teach you to dance?"

"As a matter of fact they did. It's called the bayonet two step."

Will managed not to step on Laverne's feet as they danced to a romantic song, holding each other close. When the music stopped, Laverne thanked him for the dance and complimented him. "You're a wonderful dancer now. And you're the only man I ever want to dance with." Will still had his arms around her. "And you're the only woman for me."

After both couples returned to their table from the dance floor, Frankie Ragsdale and his cohorts stopped in front of their table.

Frankie looked down at Will while speaking to his buddies. "Joe, what do you do if a Marine throws a grenade at you?" Joe had a dumb look on his face and didn't know what to say, so Frankie continued. "Pull the pin and throw it back." Joe hee-hawed even though he didn't really get it.

Frankie watched for a reaction from Will, and when he didn't get one, he spoke again to his cronies. "You wanna know what Marines are like? They're like a bunch of bananas. They start out green, then they turn yellow and die in bunches." Frankie and his friends all laughed and strutted over to the punch table.

Pete started to get up but Will stopped him saying, "No Pete. This was directed at me. And I waited eleven weeks for this."

Laverne looked frightened as Will rose alone from the table and walked confidently to the punch table. There he poured two glasses of punch without looking up. Frankie had a cocky smirk on his face as he watched Will.

With a cordial smile on his face, Will held up the glasses full of punch. "I think I should offer you some punch and settle this Frankie."

Just as Will expected, Frankie wasn't through with his insults. Frankie glared hatefully at him. "I don't drink with jungle bunnies or sea-going bell-hops."

Will looked calmly into Frankie's eyes. "Well if you insist. I guess I can let you wear it instead. Afterall, it is your turn."

Will took the glass of red punch in his right hand and threw it on Frankie's white shirt. Frankie looked down at his splattered shirt in disbelief. Will waited a moment, appreciating Frankie's dramatic expressions unfolding before he proceeded. Then Will took the punch in his left hand and threw it in Frankie's face.

Frankie responded with a fist ready to hit Will; however, Will was prepared and stopped his swing in mid air. Then Will hit Frankie so hard that Frankie flew across the floor and ended at the foot of the Clarinet player.

The musicians stopped playing and the room had become silent. Making no attempt to help, Frankie's buddies looked at Frankie as he got up and tried to steady himself while red punch dripped from his hair. Grabbing the dumbfounded musician's clarinet for a weapon, Frankie charged toward Will. Again Will was prepared for the attack. He wrung the instrument out of Frankie's hand, punched him, and knocked the wind out of him.

By now, everyone in the room was watching the activity. It was apparent to the bystanders, including Frankie's hood friends, that Will easily had the upper hand.

The musician, walked over to pick up his now sticky clarinet. He was relieved to find that no damage was done to it – but he flipped off Frankie before he rejoined his band buddies.

Frankie was livid and wouldn't give up, even though it was obvious to everyone else that he was the loser. In a last ditch effort, as Will turned to go back to the table, Frankie grabbed the huge, half-filled punch bowl in order to heave it at Will. But as he held it over his head, he lost his balance while slithering on the wet slippery floor, and Frankie fell with a mighty crash, breaking his right arm and badly cutting his left leg accidentally on the broken glass, all by his own doing.

Frankie lay on the floor as the local police came in the door. He screamed curse words and pointed at Will. "He tried to kill me." Knowing Frankie's reputation, the two police officers seemed unimpressed, and one of them said, "Ragsdale, I'd bet my paycheck that you were the trouble maker." Then he looked at his partner. "It appears somebody finally taught this spoiled rich kid a lesson."

The officers began exiting the building, supporting Frankie, who left a blood and punch drip trail all the way to the police car. One of the policemen turned around before they were out the door and smiled at the table where two handsome Marines sat with two pretty girls.

Frankie's cowardly friends were standing in the shadows outside the Legion Hall. They watched as the policemen drove away with Frankie moaning in the backseat. The thug named Joe, waited for the police car to be out of sight and then babbled. "Man, we need to blow this popcorn stand and find us some new territory. Our leader crapped out and them Marines are big trouble. I'm outta here."

The Legion Hall clean-up crew had already begun to mop up the mess, and it wasn't long before the band was playing and the dance floor was full of happy people again.

The Police report showed that Frankie Ragsdale was responsible for the disruption, the broken punchbowl, the ruined tablecloth, and they recomended that he should pay for replacement of these items, along with the cleaning of the floor.

Frankie had twelve stitches on his leg and wore a cast on his arm for three months.

20

The Shocking Truth

For several days after the incident at the Legion Hall, Will felt as if a huge weight had been lifted from his shoulders. He'd finally settled something that had been troubling him for many months; however, little did he know that he would soon have to deal with a staggering, earthshaking fact, which would also ultimately shake the world of Frankie Ragsdale.

It was revealed to him one morning after he dressed and met the family at the breakfast table. Milford and Little Becky were already waiting at the road for the school bus when he noticed his mom and dad were unusually quiet. Walter normally was already out in the fields working with Charlie, but he hadn't even put on his boots yet. Finally, he couldn't stand the silence any longer and Will asked, "Who died?"

Looking annoyed, Walter blurted, "Nobody died, Will."

Velma started to say something and then put her hand over her mouth and tears came to her eyes. She started to speak again with her hands shaking and her lips quivering. Slowly, wiping away her tears away with her apron, she resolutely continued.

"Will, your dad and I have been struggling for years as to whether or not to tell you what we are about to tell you. There are many reasons why we feel that it is right for you to know the truth now. Because you will soon be getting married, and because of the incident with your brother at the dance, this matter has been brought to our attention again."

Will appeared confused. "But...Jimmy T wasn't at the dance. And I know Milford..."

Walter interrupted, "There ain't no easy way of tellin' you this Will. But I ain't your real father."

"What are you talkin' about, Dad?"

Walter had turned pale and Velma took Walter's hand as she shared the truth with Will. "God has forgiven me for what happened over twenty years ago. And after I tell you, I hope you will forgive me, Will."

Will couldn't believe what he was hearing. He clutched the bottom of his chair with both hands until his knuckles turned white while Velma told the facts.

"Over twenty years ago, I was employed as a member of the Ragsdale household staff. We lived in the maid's quarters at the mansion when Jimmy T was a toddler. Walter was gone most of the time working their fields. This was before we became sharecroppers on our own. I don't have any excuse, but I was concerned he'd fire me if I resisted his advances. He was such a lonely man who had lost his wife—and I just gave in instead of fighting him. Walter almost killed him when he found out what had happened. Of course we quit working there and we moved, but I soon realized I was pregnant and blood tests showed us who was the father. Will, Hollis Ragsdale is your real father."

Velma was overcome with emotion and couldn't speak coherently any more. Will, stunned by what he had just been told, and trying to process the information, backed away from the table. He looked at his distraught mother and then at his agitated dad. Only, he wasn't really his dad. How could this be? Will's mind was racing. And his mother...what had she suffered?

In a burst of compassion for his mother, Will moved to her chair. Velma stood up sobbing and Will put his arms around her. Meanwhile, Walter put his head in his hands and left the room.

Will felt like a bomb had been dropped, but the aftermath showed no obvious indication of destruction like a bomb would leave – just confusion while he ran every which way inside his head, trying to find his way out of this fragile maze of truth he knew he must comprehend. There was no need to retaliate to enemy fire as he had been taught in the recent weeks. This was not the enemy. He would somehow grasp the astounding fact he had just been told, and move on...quickly, without panic.

Will attempted to console his mother and reassure her. When she quieted down, he kissed her forehead and went to find Walter.

Will found Walter in the barn, tinkering with something on his tool bench. He didn't look up at Will until Will put his arm around his shoulder and said, "You're my dad and you'll always be my dad. Nothing will ever change that." Walter couldn't hide his feelings any longer and embraced Will as they both shook with feelings.

Eventually, Will suggested that they go back to the house and drink the last of the coffee. It was quiet for a while, but eventually Will and his parents sat at the table and talked freely. Will told them he thought he should visit

Hollis Ragsdale. Then suddenly, Will blurted in realization, "Dear God. I beat up my half brother."

The next morning, Will drove to the Ragsdale estate. He'd seen the enormous plantation style home from a distance but never entered the property. The mansion was glistening white in the sun with porticos and verandahs and huge doors and windows. It was all framed in incredible land-scaping and it looked like something from the movie, "Gone With The Wind." Nevertheless, Will knew it wouldn't be Scarlet who could answer the door.

After ringing a door bell that seemed to echo like cathedral chimes, an elderly, immaculately dressed servant opened the door. Will took a deep breath and announced, "My name is Will Brown. I would like to talk to Mr. Hollis Ragsdale please."

The servant responded in a strange voice, with his chin held so high that Will wondered if he could see past his nose. The man chortled, "I shall see if he is available, Mr. Brown. Will you please come in and wait here?" The servant held out his long arm and manicured fingers to indicate a waiting area.

Will sat down to wait on a very fine settee in the massive entranceway. In a short time, the servant returned and lead Will down a wide marbled floor hallway that opened into a large study that smelled like cigars and leather. He directed him to sit in a plush chair where Will waited while watching sparks flying from a burning log inside the gigantic fireplace. Thinking he was alone in the room, Will was surprised to hear the voice of Hollis Ragsdale.

"I've done some wicked things in my life...but what I did to your mother was the worst."

Will turned around to see a handsome, silver haired man leaning on a fancy cane. Will stood up and faced him, but Hollis Ragsdale turned his back to him and continued speaking. There was a long pause between each sentence. "There's no excuse. At the time I thought there was. I'd lost my wife. I'd been drinking. I've always had a drinking problem."

Will tried to interrupt. "Mr. Ragsdale, I'm not here to..." But Hollis was determined to finish articulating what he was thinking. It had been so long in coming to the son he never knew except from a distance.

"I know you don't know me but I've watched your life. Walter hated me for a long time, but he was the best man to raise you. And you have a good mother." He rambled on, continuing in long pauses unless Will tried to interject something. Then Hollis would talk over him, as if he was fearful of what Will would say.

Will began to feel sorry for him as Hollis continued. "I can't think of one single thing in my entire life that I can be proud of. I've even failed in raising Frankie. I wish I could go back and start over, I'd do so many things differently."

Hollis sat down and stared into the fireplace. He was quiet for a moment and then said, "Will God forgive me?" Then he slowly looked up at Will and studied him. "Could you forgive me, Will Brown?"

Will kindly held out his hand and said "I forgive you Mr. Ragsdale. My mother and my fiance taught me God always forgives...if you ask Him. And I know He can give you a new start. He gave me one."

Tears rolled down Hollis Ragsdale's wrinkled face as he grasped Will's hand.

A lot had happened in Will's life since he made the decision to be a Marine, but finding out that Hollis Ragsdale was his real father and Frankie was his half brother was the most astonishing. He wondered how Frankie would feel if he knew they were related. He couldn't wait to talk to Laverne about what he'd learned.

Will had worn his uniform to the Ragsdale estate and he knew that Laverne liked to see him in his uniform. After he left the estate, he stopped at the Florist shop and bought her a bouquet of flowers on his way to the County Recorder's Office.

As he entered the office and walked confidently towards Laverne's desk, all eyes were on the handsome Marine, and one of the secretaries even whistled at him. As all the office staff watched and listened, Will placed the flowers on her desk and asked her in a gallant voice, "Oh beautiful woman of my dreams, will you have lunch with me?"

Laverne giggled and agreed to lunch, whereupon Will swept her off her feet and carried her out the door as the employees laughed.

When Laverne stopped giggling, she asked, "What happened to my shy boyfriend I used to know?"

Will kissed her lips. "Somebody must have prayed for me."

Will and Laverne sat at their favorite table in the back corner of Ruth's

Café. Sally Springer waited on them and the couple ordered cheese burgers, fries and chocolate milkshakes.

Sally complimented Will, "Pete and I are really proud of you, Will. You really let that Ragsdale punk know what's what!" Will smiled at Sally, but in his heart, it bothered him to think about his half brother.

After Laverne finished eating, she gave the remainder of her milkshake to Will. "I won't fit in my wedding dress if I keep eating like this."

Will took the milkshake from her but he insisted, "Ah come on. A breeze could blow you away." Then he changed the subject. "You'll never believe where I've been this morning. I've just found out something that will blow your mind. I've learned that Hollis Ragsdale is my real father."

Will watched Laverne, expecting her to be shocked, but Will was the one who was taken aback at her unruffled response.

"I know."

"What do you mean you know? How do you know?"

"One day at work, I was looking for some old records to copy, and by chance, I found out."

"Why didn't you tell me?"

"It wasn't my place to tell you, Will. I wanted to tell you, but it wasn't right. Don't you understand that? Besides, it doesn't change my love for you."

"You don't care that I'm really a Ragsdale?"

"Walter adapted you, so you're really a Brown. And I want to be Mrs. Brown. Besides, I wouldn't care if your name was mud. Which mine will be if you don't get me back to work on time."

That night, Will thought about the events of the day. Despite what he had learned about his real father, he had peace about it. He thanked his mother and dad for telling him the facts, and he reassured them again. He finally figured out why Walter always seemed distant to him. The circumstances of his conception had caused, not only his mom, but his dad tremendous pain. Although Walter had tried to forgive Hollis Ragsdale later in his life, a root of bitterness had robbed him of joy.

Admitting the truth of Ragsdale's fatherhood had been a breakthrough for everyone. Also, since Will told Walter, "You're my dad and you'll always be my dad. Nothing will ever change that," there was a new warmth in Walter, and their relationship was thriving at last.

Velma had carried a burden of guilt for not telling Will that Walter wasn't his father. The weight of it was gone at last, and the entire family basked in the sweet spirit that had descended on the household. Indeed, the truth had set them free.

21

The Wedding

Every pew in the First Assembly of God Church was filled on the evening of December 1st. The sanctuary was adorned with red roses and candles and large white bows at the end of every pew.

As the audience waited for the wedding ceremony, The parents and families of the bride and groom were ushered into the front left or right rows, depending on whether they were friends or family of the bride or of the groom. There was whispering among people who were curious at seeing Hollis Ragsdale, proudly seated in the front row beside Walter Brown.

When everyone was seated, Pete Springer's girl friend, Latoya, sang "Amazing Grace," inviting the congregation to sing with her. Many of the Pentecostal audience lifted their hands in praise to God, including the two men in the front row on the groom's side. It wasn't exactly a traditional wedding ceremony, but everyone felt an unusually strong presence of love and joy.

When the singing was finished, Pete Springer, who was Will's best man, and five other Marines from Platoon 101, came to the front of the church and stood with Will, all dressed in striking Marine dress blue uniforms.

The bridesmaids and the flower girl, all in light blue taffeta dresses, came up the aisle one at a time as the guest organist, Laverne's Uncle Bob from Oregon, skillfully played the glorious Trumpet Voluntary. After a short pause, and all the attendants were in place, Uncle Bob played the traditional Bridal Chorus and everyone stood up and turned to look at the Bride coming up the aisle.

Looking more beautiful than ever in her long, white bridal gown and train, Laverne walked slowly to the altar, keeping her sparkling eyes on Will. She held a bouquet of long stemmed red roses and a delicate lacey veil covered her head and face.

When Laverne reached the front, and still had her back to the audience, the organist stopped playing and Pastor Dan stepped forward and told the congregation what he and Laverne had discussed for the ceremony.

"As you can see, no one has escorted our dear Laverne down the aisle on this, her wedding day. There is no person here to give her away—as tradition normally has it. However, I've known Laverne since she was born, and I baptised her in this church. I also know that although her human father, who doesn't live in this state, chose not to be here, her Heavenly Father is here to give her to Will Brown, to be his cherished wife.

At that point, Pastor Dan turned and took Laverne's hand, and helped her to move beside Will. Laverne's cousin, Cheryl, took the bridal bouquet from Laverne so her hands would be free, and Will and Laverne joined hands.

Pastor Dan continued, "On behalf of the Lord God of Creation and Laverne Aldeman's Savior, Jesus Christ, I hereby give her away to you, Will Brown."

Pastor Dan then moved up a step behind the couple and asked for the congregation to bow their heads in prayer.

When the vows had been said, the rings exchanged and the wedding ceremony was finished, Pastor Dan presented Mr. and Mrs. Will Brown to the congregation and they all applauded while Will kissed the bride. The organist played Mendelssohn's Wedding March and the couple and their attendants moved from the front, down the aisle to the music.

All of the Marine's wanted to kiss the bride, and hugs and handshakes were abundant. The bridal party spent at least forty minutes in the receiving line in the vestibule of the church before going to the Legion Hall for the reception.

As everyone arrived at the Legion Hall, Little Becky passed out hand-made party favors that Laverne's mother, Nina Alderman had prepared.

Charlie Shipman was in charge of the barbecue and someone said Hollis Ragsdale had supplied enough steaks "to feed an army." Someone else laughed and said, "You mean, feed the Marine Corps, not the Army."

Sally Springer and all the crew from Ruth's Café helped to serve the large crowd an unforgettable meal. The Bridal party was served first as they sat at a long table at the head of the room.

When everyone had been served and had eaten all they wanted, Pete Springer tapped his water glass with a spoon to get everyone's attention. He toasted the bride and the groom and told a silly story about Will, making everyone laugh. Then he asked various people to stand up and give Will and Laverne some marital advice—which many did. It started out with an attitude of seriousness, but soon the funny suggestions that were made had people roaring with laughter.

The local Western band supplied the music, and Milford surprised everyone by joining them and playing his guitar. Will and Laverne first danced alone in the center of the room with the spot light on them, and after the first song was over, others joined them. Will danced with his mother and then Nina Alderman, and Walter and Hollis Ragsdale took turns dancing with Laverne. This was followed by many who tapped the shoulder of Laverne's current dance partner to cut in so they could also dance with the beautiful bride.

Wedding gifts were stacked on a large table near the wedding cake. When it was time to cut the cake, cameras were ready. Laverne seemed to have the upper hand when she and Will shared the cake with each other. After she stuffed his face with a piece of cake, the icing made Will look as if he had a beard, but he retaliated and gave Laverne a mustache. The audience was delighted when Jimmy T insisted that Will should lick Laverne's face clean. The cameras flashed as Will obliged his brother, and the couple ended their clowning with more dancing as the band played a love song that Elvis Presley had made popular.

Later that evening, Jimmy T asked Will to go out to the parking lot with him for a minute. Outdoors, he handed Will the keys to a new-looking, green Pontiac. Jimmy T explained, "A fella owed me money and asked me if I'd take the car instead. I knew you needed a car, so since this one had low mileage and was in good shape, I decided to get it for you."

After all that Jimmy T had already done to help with the cost of the wedding, Will was almost speechless. He grabbed his brother and embraced him. "I love you Jimmy T. Thank you."

Laverne was sitting with her mother and Velma when the brothers came back inside. When Will told her about the car, she hugged her brother-in-law and thanked him. Walter overheard the conversation and he shook hands with Jimmy T. "Son, you've been very generous to us. I'm proud of you."

Jimmy T was taken aback at his father's comment as he saw a change in his attitude. At that moment, Milford interrupted them and insisted that they go outside with him. He'd prepared a "JUST MARRIED" sign and a long string of tin cans. He needed their help in attaching them to the Pontiac, so Walter and Jimmy T followed Milford back outside.

After they had everything in place, and before they went back indoors, Jimmy T spoke to his dad privately.

"Dad, I've wanted to tell you this for a long time. I'm sorry I deserted you to do my own thing. Since Will is leaving, I'm willing to give up everything and return to the farm if you need me."

Walter looked down at the ground solemnly. "You don't have to do that son. I haven't treated you or Will right. Forgive me for being selfish. It takes something like this wedding for a man to realize that to love and be loved is as good as it gets, this side of Heaven."

Sally Springer caught the bridal bouquet when Laverne threw it to a group of giggling single women. And when Will produced the garter that Laverne had worn, one of his Marine buddies named Jack, caught it. He just happened to be the man that Sally had her eye on, and she was glad when he asked her to dance. As it turned out, six months later, Jack and Sally eloped.

Will and Laverne opened their many wedding gifts before the reception party was over. It was almost midnight when they finally said their goodbyes and thank yous to everyone.

Little Becky, Milford, and all their friends had hand fulls of rice ready to throw at the bride and groom when they walked out the door to their new car.

Everyone waved as the green Pontiac pulled out of the parking lot with a noisy clanging.

22

Getting Things Settled

For their honeymoon, Will and Laverne rented a cottage in Virginia Beach. Will carried Laverne in his arms over the threshold, and once they unpacked and got comfortable, they enjoyed each other so much, they hardly left the cottage on the first two days of their stay. On the third day of their honeymoon, the newlyweds finally decided to venture out and see the sights, and the remaining five days were filled with fun as they explored the area.

One day they went to Mantage and checked out the shops. After buying a couple souvenirs at the mall, they went down to the beach. Blissful with their love for each other, they played on the beach like children, building sand castles, chasing each other along the shore, picking up shells and behaving like the elated young lovers that they were. At night they enjoyed romantic, candle light dinners at the Beachcomber Restaurant.

Their unforgetable week flew past and it became time for them to report to the base at Camp Lejeune in North Carolina for base housing.

When they arrived at Camp Lejeune, Will and Laverne were given a map of the base which showed everything on the property including the commissary, the PX, the hospital and the pharmacy. There was an X marked on the map showing the location of their new residence. Along with a set of keys and some paperwork for Will, Laverne was surprised when she was issued an ID card.

"Why do I need this?"

Will explained, "You need the card in order to get into the commissary and the various facilities."

Laverne thanked the officer that handed her the ID card and smiled. "I'm beginning to feel like a Marine. Now I'm wondering if there is a job available for me on the base."

A MP overheard her comment as he walked by and responded, "Mrs. Brown, being a Marine's wife is the toughest job in the Corps!"

Laverne looked at Will and said, "Well, if that's the worst job, I've got it made."

Then the clerk behind the desk handed Laverne a job application. In the weeks following, she was given a job at the Post Exchange.

Their housing accommodations were very basic at Camp Lejeune, but because of their love for each other, it wouldn't have mattered if they lived in a tent. Laverne had spent a day arranging things and had made it look very homey. Only one more touch for the wall over the couch while she waited for her husband to come home from an orientation. She hung the little plaque on the wall that her mother had given them as a wedding gift. It read:

Trust in the lord with all thine heart and lean not unto thine own understanding. In all thy ways acknowledge him, and he shall direct thy paths. (Proverbs 3:5-6).

"There," she said out loud as she positioned it, "Perfect." And at the same time, Will walked in the door.

"Who are you talking to honey?"

"Myself. That way I get the answers I want."

Will laughed and hugged her. "I'm learning something new about you every day. And now I've learned you talk to yourself. But I'm glad we're alone. I couldn't wait to get home to be with you."

Will started to lead her to the other room when Laverne noticed the letters in his hand. "Who are those from?"

Will looked at the return address on one of the envelopes which he hadn't noticed before. He didn't recognize the name, Jim Davis/Esquire. After opening the envelope, he became aware that the letter was from Hollis Ragsdale's lawyer.

Will's demeanor changed as he read the letter. Then he sat down on the couch and looked at the floor. "Well, I didn't have very much opportunity to get to know my real father. Hollis Ragsdale was found dead in his den."

Laverne sat down beside Will. The two were silent for a while and then Will said, "The letter said that Mr. Davis is the executor of Hollis' estate and has requested my presence at the reading of his will."

A month later, Will was given leave to attend the reading of Hollis Ragsdale's Last Will and Testimony, so Will and Laverne found themselves back in their home town, surprising their friends and relatives with their early return.

While they were in town, they stayed in Laverne's old bedroom at Nina Alderman's home. And when Will went to hear the reading, Laverne stayed and visited with her mom until he came back.

The law offices of Jim Davis were in an impressive brick building. The waiting room had several, large leather couches, brass lamps and expensive looking furnishings. Original oil paintings hung on the wall and magazines were arranged on the coffee tables.

Will found Frankie Ragsdale seated in the room and smoking a cigarette when he arrived. His feet were crossed with the heels of his boots resting on the coffee table. When Frankie saw Will, he put his feet on the floor, put out his cigarette, and defensively glared at Will.

Will walked towards him and held out his hand. "Frankie, I think it's time we put away our differences." But before Frankie made any attempt at responding, the dignified lawyer, Jim Davis, came into the waiting room and invited the men into his office, so Frankie turned around without acknowledging Will's suggestion.

Jim Davis sat at one side of a large oak table and Will and Frankie sat on the other side. A secretary offered the men coffee and poured it, then she sat at the end of the table where she recorded the proceedings on a tape recorder.

The lawyer began with a serious, formal manner. "Gentlemen, this is a legal document, properly recorded and notarized. Your father made it very clear what he wanted, and if you choose to benefit from his generous decisions, you will abide by his wishes. Normally, I would not comment with personal opinion, or become personally involved in matters such as this; however, Hollis had my respect and admiration and I am proud to say he trusted me to see that his desires would be carried out. He was my friend."

"I believe that you will both appreciate what I'm about to relate." The lawyer looked directly at Frankie, who was scowling. "If not immediately, some day you will see the wisdom in this document. Now I'll begin."

"'I, Hollis Ragsdale, being of sound mind and without reservations do declare that upon my death, everything I own shall be distributed as written herein.

To Will Brown, I will the sharecropper farm which Walter Brown and his family have lived and managed for many years, and also one hundred eighty acres surrounding the property.'"

Frankie shook his head in disgust as an amazed Will put his head into his hands and thought about what joy this would bring to all the Brown family.

"'To my son, Frankie Ragsdale, I will the remainder of my estate...'"

Frankie pointed two thumbs up, nodded and smirked, but the lawyer hadn't yet read the stipulations.

"'...with the condition that Frankie serves four years honorably in the United States Marine Corps. If he fails to serve within five years of my death, or in the case of his own death, the entire estate will go to Will Brown.'"

Will gasped and Frankie furiously pounded the table with his fists. The lawyer closed the document and musingly considered the stark difference in demeanor of both men.

Frankie stood up and cursed. As he exited the room, he mumbled, "I'm glad the old bastard is dead."

Laverne, her mother and all the members of the Brown family and friends were elated to hear of Will's good fortune. The paperwork was quickly processed and Will's name was placed on the deed to the sharecroppers farm and the 180 acres surrounding it. Also, Will had asked Jim Davis to draw up a document that would insure deed ownership to his family members in case anything happened to him.

Walter Brown was overjoyed with the new possibilities for the farm. Not wanting to take advantage of his son's prosperity, he insisted on an agreement pertaining to the profits gained through harvesting the land. Then he hired four men to work under the supervision of Charlie Shipman.

Velma began preparations for a celebration dinner before Will and Laverne had to return to the base. With so many folks coming to congratulate Will, it ended up being a potluck, and the small farmhouse was filled with merriment on the evening before Will and Laverne went back to the base.

Will and Laverne had said their goodbyes to everyone and promised to write. The couple happily discussed their dreams for the future as they drove down the highway in their green Pontiac. They spoke of owning their own home and having children—and now they felt they could begin to prepare financially for that day.

23

Compliance

Realizing that he had no choice if he wanted to enjoy his inheritance, Frankie Ragsdale begrudgingly submitted to his father's demands as they were stipulated in the will. Downcast and pessimistic, he enlisted in the Marines, and in a few months, Frankie arrived at Parris Island.

Frankie's resentment was clearly seen on his face as he stepped off the Marine bus. Lining up with the other recruits, he saw what he perceived as a very annoying child standing in front of them. The red-haired kid was wearing a miniature, green Marine uniform and he stood proudly beside a rather intimidating, red-haired sergeant who was speaking in an icy voice.

"I am Staff Sergeant Kohler. This is my son, Victor. You will also become acquainted with Sergeant Jakobowski and Sergeant Wrobelski who will be assisting me for the next eleven weeks. You will remember that anytime you wish to speak to us it will be preceded by 'Sir' and will end with 'Sir.' Is that understood?"

The recruits responded. "Sir, yes Sir."

Kohler continued, "Reveille will be at four-thirty. You will have fifteen minutes to shit, shave, shower and shampoo; thirty minutes to get in and out of the chow hall; fifteen minutes to make your beds, clean your quarters, dress and be outside in three ranks by five-thirty. Is that understood?"

When all the usual instructions were given, Kohler made eye contact with Frankie who had been frowning. The sergeant always had a keen perceptivity about his recruits. He'd seen a hundred just like Frankie arriving with an attitude; yet, Kohler still found each personality a challenge and looked forward to his part in their transformation.

Kohler stepped directly in front of Frankie with an expression on his face that would melt candle wax. Less than an inch from his face, Kohler yelled at him. "State your name and where you are from."

Frankie swallowed and his frown disappeared. "Sir, Frankie Ragsdale, Beckley, West Virginia, Sir."

Sergeant Wrobelski followed behind Kohler. Sniffing Frankie, Wrobelski screeched, "You smell sweet. You have a feminine voice and a fair complexion. Your smell and your voice betray you, and your beer belly doesn't fit with your skinny legs."

That night after lights were out, Frankie Ragsdale tossed and turned on his bunk and ran his hands over his newly shaved head. He considered the possibility of leaving the island during the night, but then he would lose everything that rightfully belonged to him. He cursed loudly into his pillow. Three or four voices in the darkness yelled at him using various phrases including, "Shut up and go to sleep Ragsdale!"

24

The Brig

Friends since their childhood, Will Brown and Pete Springer enjoyed it when they found themselves in some of the same training drills on the base. And they were glad to hear that they would both be going to Little Creek, Virginia for one week of Amphibious Training.

One night Pete and some friends decided to go to Virginia Beach and check out a bar they'd heard about. Knowing that partying would make it too hard to get up and be ready for training in the morning, Will didn't go with them, and instead he went to bed. But he was awakened by Joe Murdoch a little after midnight.

Murdoch's breath and manner made it clear he had too much to drink as he told Will, "Spring...er's real...ly drunk!"

Will sat up in bed and looked at the tottering messenger swaying beside his bunk. "Where is he?"

Murdoch, held out his arm and pointed west with his hand before it dropped to his side. "Motel Six, rooom nine-ty one!"

Concerned that his friend wouldn't make roll call, Will dressed and took a taxi to the Motel. When he arrived, he saw that the door of room 91 was cracked open. He could see Pete sitting on the side of the bed, masturbating. Will kicked the door open wide and blurted, "Springer! What in the hell do you think you're doing?"

Blurry-eyed and unsteady, Pete looked towards the doorway. "Will, I'm so drunk, I don't even know who I'm fucking."

Will put Pete with his clothes still on in a cold shower. After Pete was somewhat sobered up, he managed to get him back to the base. But Pete's reckless escapades continued for a while.

Two weeks later, Pete and Johnny Driscoll sat drinking beer at Sam's Bar in Kinston, North Carolina that was often populated by servicemen. They were reminiscing about their wild experiences at Parris Island when an eavesdropping, drunk sailor began making rude remarks about Marines. He asked, "Are there any sea-going bellhops around?"

Finally, Pete had enough of the sailor's insulting comments. It was clear the sailor was obviously trying to provoke him, so he grabbed the earring in the sailor's ear and ripped it off, leaving the man with a bleeding ear. The drunk sailor attempted to swing at Pete, but Pete was ready. He ducked in time and pushed the sailor down on the bar with his hands around his neck, terrifying the bartender, but Johnny Driscol looked at the bartender and calmly explained, "Don't worry, Sir, it's his family tradition." Then Driscol turned around and threw his drink in the face of an approaching sailor who held a club in his hand.

A brawl broke out after these interchanges. Punches were thrown, chairs broken and glasses shattered on the floors as the frenzied crowd of servicemen fought. Eventually, MP's took control of the situation and the bar was cleared out. Pete and Driscoll were escorted back to Camp Lejeune by the Marine Military Police. Both had black eyes and bruises, and were locked in the brig, forced to remain in cold, concrete cells for ten days.

The Warden, a moody Gunnery Sergeant, normally kept a close eye on Pete. Pete's mother had sent him a package in the mail, and he was supposed to open any mail he received in front of the Warden. It turned out to be a large box of Pete's mother's homemade chocolate chip cookies, Pete's favorite treat. Since the Warden became distracted before he opened the box and didn't see what it was, Pete quickly hid them under the cot.

The Gunny had been distracted watching a large Bulldog outside the window. The dog was the brig mascot and the animal wore a jacket. For their amusement, every time Camp Lejeune won a football game, the MPs and the sergeant would promote him, and every time they lost, they would demote him.

As the warden looked out the window, the Bulldog hiked his leg and pissed on the flagpole, infuriating the sergeant. He was livid with anger and screamed for someone to get the Bulldog and put him in the brig, so their mascot was placed behind bars with Pete. Then the gunny irrationally gave the dog, "Five days piss and punk," which means five days bread and water.

Soon after the dog was locked up with Pete, he found the chocolate chip cookies under the cot and devoured them, despite Pete's attempt to inconspicuously retrieve them.

When the warden came back to check on Pete the next morning, he was furious, suspicious that someone had fed the dog. The fat on the Bulldog's belly was unusually bulging. Looking suspiciously at Pete, he watched him more closely than ever.

The remaining days in the brig were miserable for Pete. He was forced to sleep on the floor because whenever he came near the bunk, the Bulldog showed his teeth and growled.

When Pete was released from the brig, he vowed to his friends that he was through with drinking. He'd had a lot of time to sit on the concrete floor and think about his life – and he finally realized that whenever he got drunk, he got into trouble. When the Chaplain visited the brig, Pete had a long conversation with him. Before the minister left, he and the Chaplain prayed that God would deliver Pete from alcoholism. And He did.

25

Announcement

Laverne had prepared a special dinner before Will came home. After he had his shower, he found her lighting two candles in the middle of the dinner table. Her face glowed in the candlelight and she looked especially beautiful. He sat down and watched her as she served him his dinner, an appealing meal of lamb chops, creamed peas, rice pilaf, buttered rolls and a fruit salad. He'd already spotted her homemade apple pie, partly uncovered with a cloth, sitting on the counter and saved for dessert.

"What's the occasion, Laverne? This looks great."

"I have a surprise for you...after dinner."

Although Will was curious, he turned his attention to the irresistible dinner in front of him. They ate their dinner quietly, being so comfortable with each other that sometimes they found they didn't require words.

After they were finished eating, Will stood up to help Laverne clear the table. They piled the dirty dishes in the sink and then Will took Laverne in his arms and beamed like a little boy. "Okay. I'm ready. Where's my surprise?"

Laverne slowly removed Will's arms from around her waist, and then watching his face so she could remember the moment forever, she laid his hands on her abdomen.

"Your surprise is right here. I'm pregnant."

Laverne was a few months along when one evening, as she stood at the sink washing dishes, she felt the baby move. Will had been particularly attentive to Laverne since he learned of the pregnancy, so when he saw her suddenly stop what she was doing, he panicked. "What's wrong?"

Laverne broke out in a smile and asked him to feel the baby moving with his hand. Will was overcome with the experience of feeling the life of his child. His face took on a comical, bewildered expression and he stuttered. "How...how...what's happening?"

Laverne laughed hard at his reaction and tears ran down her face. She shook her head. "Well, I didn't swallow a watermelon seed. The baby kicked."

Will knelt down beside his wife and put his ear to her belly. "Hello, little Will. This is your daddy speaking."

Laverne laughed some more and advised, "Daddy, you know you could be talking to a little Laverne."

The grandparents rejoiced at hearing the good news, but the couple had waited almost five months before they made an announcement concerning their baby-to-be to anyone else. Since Laverne couldn't hide her pregnancy any longer, they decided to have a party and make an announcement to their neighbors and friends on the base.

On the morning of the party, Laverne went to the commissary and picked up paper plates and groceries needed for the party, and then she spent part of the afternoon preparing things.

Will prepared the yard for their guests with a makeshift table that had a plywood top covered with a plastic table cloth. Some sturdy benches made of tree stumps and well-worn boards were used for seating.

Will barbecued hot dogs for everyone that evening, and when Pete Springer arrived, he helped Laverne carry things to the table. Laverne brought out the large macaroni salad she'd prepared and placed it on the table beside a bowl potato chips, a pitcher of iced tea and the mustard and ketchup.

As Pete helped bring other items from the house, he found a plate of homemade peanut butter cookies in the kitchen and was sneaking them before dinner. He happened to notice a bottle sitting on the counter that had the words "Prenatal Vitamins" written on the label. He chuckled, thinking he'd accidentally discovered what the party was all about.

After their guests arrived and everyone had finished eating, Will and Laverne told the group about their baby-to-be. The group applauded the couple and responded with words of congratulations. One of Laverne's new girlfriends asked her if she could host a baby shower in a few months. Another one of her neighbors, who already had a ten-month old baby, offered some baby clothes that had only been worn a short time since babies grow so fast. Pete hugged Will and told him he knew he would be a good father. Then he told Will that he also had an announcement.

Pete had a serious look on his face. Taking Will aside so that no one could hear him, he told him, "In two weeks, my unit is replacing a regiment in Vietnam. I haven't told my folks yet, but I wanted you to know." Will knew very bad things were happening in Vietnam and his first reaction was fear for his friend. But he suppressed the negative feeling he had, and responded with saying, "Thanks for letting me know, Pete. You're a close friend and I'll miss you."

There was silence between the two and then Will ordered cheerfully, "Go over there and show 'em how West Virginia boys can fight!"

The barbecue party was a huge success. It was the beginnings of new relationships and acquaintances with people who would end up being their dearest friends for the rest of their lives.

As Will and Laverne cleaned up after the party, Laverne commented, "You know Will, not only has the Marine Corps built your character and enriched your life with special people, it's also been a great blessing to me."

Will kissed Laverne's cheek as he uncovered the plate which once held peanut butter cookies. He looked aghast at the empty plate, then at Laverne. Then at the exact same time the couple nodded their heads at each other and mouthed the name, "Pete."

Will sighed, "Well...I can't be mad at him. He told me tonight that his unit is leaving for Vietnam. It'll be a while before I see him. But when I do..."

Laverne interrupted, "Oh no. This is scary news. Is there a chance you'll have to go before the baby is born?"

"Let's set our mind on possibilities instead of probabilities, and pray. I think we need to plan on what we should do if I get orders, Laverne."

26

Camp Pendleton

Several weeks after Pete Springer's unit landed in Vietnam, Will's unit received orders to report to Camp Pendleton in California for Guerilla Warfare School. Will and Laverne had decided it would be best for Laverne to return to Beckley and stay with her mother. Of course, Nina Alderman was delighted. The government moved the couple's possessions to Beckley for them and their things would be stored in Nina's garage.

Although Laverne was not looking forward to returning without Will, at least she had already been promised that she could have her old job back at the Raleigh County Recorder's office until the baby was born. That would help her to pass the time while they were apart.

Laverne walked alongside Will as he headed for the gate to board the C130 flight for Camp Pendleton and she began to cry quietly. "Please come back Will. We need you."

Will stopped walking, and with one last embrace and kiss, coaxed her in a voice that came out hoarsely, "God will see us through this." He tried his best to be a comfort to Laverne. Meanwhile, his heart was beating faster than usual, partly because he had never flown before.

Laverne was still weeping when the C130 kicked in its after burners and astoundingly took off in less than 300 yards.

The Camp Pendleton base didn't look much different from the Marine bases on the other side of the United States—except for the fact that a portion of the property was a replica of a Vietnamese village. Everything there had been constructed for training and it included water buffalos, dogs and chickens.

The Commanding Officer, Captain Russ Soehner informed the company they would be flying to Okinawa, Japan after their training in California, and orders beyond Okinawa were Top Secret.

The weather was gorgeous, and although most of the men had a dark California tan by the time they finished training, they weren't there for the weather. The Commanding Officer made no bones about it. They were there precisely to learn how to keep from being killed while aggressively defending their country. Every hour spent would be training to that end.

The training was based on a three point philosophy of the renowned guerrilla fighter, Father Ho:

1. He that does not know himself or his enemy will be defeated in every battle.
2. He that knows himself but not his enemy will suffer one defeat for every victory.
3. He that knows himself and his enemy will be victorious in every battle.

The men were taught that the French were defeated in Vietnam because they tried to fight using typical, conventional approaches for what they thought was a typical war although they were warring against an irregular, guerrilla enemy. They learned how the French gravely underestimated the home field advantage of the Viet Cong; how it rained daily in Vietnam, causing the humidity to be very high, and causing thirst and possible dehydration. They learned that the French were sold drinks by vendors on the side of the road, not learning until later as they bled in the hospital that the drinks had ground glass in them.

Another experience was related about a French convoy that was hit. The soldiers dived for cover, only to find that the ditches they dived into had poisoned punji sticks placed in them. There were crude devises made from a notch of bamboo, a nail and a 12 gauge shotgun shell that had the potential to blow a man's foot off if he stepped on it.

They were taught the many tactics of their enemy. They learned the importance of caution and not taking the "easy way," which would be tempting, but that way might be deadly. Trails, for instance, were to be avoided and they must always look for signs and clues indicating the proximity of the enemy. When entering a village, they were told to beware, especially if there were no barking dogs. They were informed about the vast network of tunnels, tunnel entrances under water and tunnel rat training. Among other things, the men became knowledgeable about the particulars of setting up base camps, using trained dogs, and how to identify poisonous snakes.

They were warned that the ARVIN, the South Vietnamese Army, had been infiltrated by the Viet Cong, and in some cases, got off a helicopter merely to throw a hand grenade back into the chopper.

Everyone was given a copy of the book *Street Without Joy*, which was the sobering story about the French occupation and Highway One.

Along with many dedicated young Marines, Will Brown found experiences at Camp Pendleton challenging. During the first part of training, Will was appalled to hear one of the referees who had been monitoring the training tell him, "Brown, you've been 'killed' sixteen times." Later that night when he compared notes with others, he found out that everyone had been "killed" a lot and didn't feel quite so devastated. Still, the thought that one small mistake could leave his wife a widow was distressing.

Although Will had once thought nothing could be harder than Parris Island, this training was harder in a different way. And this was because he realized more and more that all the information they were teaching him, and every move he needed to learn, could someday save his life or the life of others.

Will had no idea what the future would bring or where he would be sent after Okinawa. But he did know he wanted to live to be an old man with his precious wife and child, to eventually go back home to Beckley and live a life, unconcerned about war.

That night on his cot, He prayed more than usual.

27

Semper Fidelis

The last two words Captain Russ Soehner solemnly spoke to the Marine company before they saluted him and boarded the C130 for Okinawa were, "Semper Fidelis," the Latin phrase meaning, "Always faithful."

Every bucket seat was occupied on the airplane when at the last minute before the engines rumbled, a fuel truck was driven into the airplane and battened down. Then surprisingly, three more Marines entered the plane and were seated in the front seat of the truck. Every square inch seemed to be efficiently used for transporting soldiers or equipment. Nevertheless, after the C130 taxied down the runway, it took off with remarkable ease, impressing Will Brown with its incredible power.

Camp Hansen in Okinawa, Japan was the plane's destination, and when they arrived, they were told they would only be there for two days. This was the first foreign country Will had ever been in, and he and a few of his Marine friends decided to check out the town on the first night.

As they walked through the colorful and noisy streets of Okinawa, Will immediately noticed the contrast between the service clubs on the main side. The Air Force Club was like a Las Vegas resort with valet parking, women in elegant evening gowns, entertainers in tuxedos, and popular America music. Down the hill from the Air Force Club stood a dirty Quonset Hut with a flashing red and gold sign that read, The Snake Pit. It was the Marine staff NCO club.

Will and his buddies bought a few oriental souvenirs, observed the Japanese people's polite manner, listened to their language, tasted their food and drinks, and got their eyes full as they walked through the intriguing streets of Japan. But in the back of all their minds was a tormenting question. Where would they be in three days?

28

Danang

They left Okinawa in a C130 incredibly packed with even more supplies than the first flight. Will Brown thought of Pete Springer and his cans of sardines. The current situation reminded him of Pete's cans of smelly fish because the plane was packed tightly with soldiers and Marines. And like those horrid cans of sardines with which Pete stunk up the Beckley Sav-A-Lot break room, the interior of the plane also had an odor...and it smelled like fear.

After what seemed like forever, the Marines were at last informed that they would be landing in a dangerous combat area. They were going to Danang, South Vietnam.

In attempt to keep from being shot down, the pilot had to keep the aircraft at a safe altitude until they were almost above the airstrip. Then suddenly, the plane dove down to make a combat landing with the passengers holding on for dear life. Will wasn't the only soldier praying because they thought they were going to crash.

The plane seemed to hit the airstrip with a bounce, but reversed its engines and came to a safe stop. Will wiped the sweat that had accumulated on his brow, began breathing again and followed the line of relieved men out the door. Their relief quickly turned to horror as they witnessed over 100 black body bags on trailers, waiting to be loaded on the plane as the company exited the aircraft. Then it began to rain. Along with the soft and pure sound of the raindrops making puddles on the ground, there was the sound of loud explosions in the distance, causing people to begin running to safe bunkers.

The city of Danang was not far from the base. On one side of the town was Hill 327 which had a Hawk Missile Battery on top of the hill. Below 327 was the Marine headquarters and the field hospital. On the other side of the city and the air base was Monkey Mountain. This was where a Seabee construction battalion which was leveling off the top of the mountain for another Hawk Missile Battery.

Will found it interesting that the ground in Vietnam was red. Unlike the good dirt at home in West Virginia, Vietnam dirt reminded him of Georgia clay.

Most Marines in the area could be found at Marble Mountain, which wasn't actually a mountain but rather two pillars of rock. And all the land beyond the Danang River was Viet Cong controlled territory.

The company that Will was in temporarily set up in a small fort that the French had built near the base. It was similar to an old western fort, but instead of logs, it was built with white cement. There were towers on all four corners and a huge wooden entrance door. They built sand bag bunkers and barbed wired was put on the outer perimeter.

A mote, surrounded the fort, and eventually the dead trees and debris that were in it were cleaned out. Will helped with this task and when the men finished cleaning out the mote, they were appalled to find filthy leaches sticking to their legs and body.

One day, the sergeant in charge of motor transport took Will on a reconnaissance trip to Monkey Mountain. Upon returning to the fort, on the outskirts of Danang, a thin, shabbily dressed Asian boy suddenly appeared from behind a building. He angrily threw something the size of a grenade into the jeep, landing behind the seats of the sergeant and Will. The men immediately bailed out of the jeep to protect themselves. Meanwhile, the jeep crashed into a small store building. A little later, when there was no explosion, they found a potato in the jeep.

Will soon came to the conclusion that potential danger could be found everywhere in this God-forsaken country, and the demeanor on the faces of every homesick serviceman expressed a wearisome cautiousness.

Even the local children couldn't always be trusted. Most of them were just friendly, resourceful kids who used the war as an opportunity to get money and gifts from the servicemen, but there had been dangerous incidents when the youngsters were ruthlessly used by the enemy.

There was an enterprising Vietnamese teenager who smilingly provided his services by washing clothes and cleaning and polishing boots for a small fee. Everyone jokingly called him VC, short for Viet Cong. He seemed trustworthy to the Marines, but one learned it was dangerous to be too trusting of anyone in this unpredictable war.

There was a small village about a half mile from the fort that the

Marines named, Dog Patch. Private George Henderson, who had a child of his own back in the States, had compassion for the children who lived in the war zone.

Late one afternoon he took candy for the kids at Dog Patch. He was shot in the back and killed.

Despite the moments of grief which regularly troubled the soldiers in Vietnam, there were individuals who seemed to have an supernatural ability to bring cheer to the troops. In retrospect, Will often wondered if his company had occasionally been visited by "Angels unaware" that he had heard about when he was a child.

Will was pretty sure, Jimmy Bunnel, who everyone called "Skinny Guinea," was no angel, but he sure could make a fella laugh. Catastrophe seemed to follow him. For instance, after he set up trip flares, he stumbled into them and set them all off. Another time he accidentally discharged his 45 and blew up his air mat.

Bunnel and Will were responsible for taking the water trailer to Monkey Mountain where the Seabees were leveling and preparing the ground for a missle sight. One day Will was driving back down the narrow mountain road when Bunnel fell asleep and fell out of the truck. He screamed as his body rolled and tumbled down a steep incline, stopping on a ragged edged boulder at about twenty feet. Will immediately stopped the truck and climbed down the rocky edge. Then he carried the injured, moaning Bunnel back up to the truck and drove him to the Danang field hospital. Eventually a helicopter flew him to an Army hospital, thirty miles south of Danang.

Since Bunnel was the only Marine in the Army hospital, he was too embarrassed to tell them that he had merely fallen out of the water truck. Instead, he claimed that he'd been captured and tortured mercilessly by the Viet Cong.

There was a Army soldier in the hospital bed beside Bunnel who was deeply moved by the details of Bunnel's supposed capture. Enjoying the attention, Bunnel continued to lie and elaborate on the fictional saga, bringing his roomate to intense compassion. The attentive soldier, who had to use crutches due to an injury to his foot, felt so bad for the poor, bedridden Marine that he hobbled around bringing him things like Cokes and cigarettes at his every bidding. It was about a week into his dedicated servanthood, when he was told the truth.

Skinny Guinea was flown out of the Army hospital to keep him from being killed. He tried to explain what happened to any Marines who'd listen. "It began with this insane cripple beating me over the head with his crutches. Then I think the whole United States Army was after my ass. I just don't understand it..."

There were other entertaining characters with whom Will became acquainted. Staff Sergeant Ted Mercer, was no angel either, but the bowlegged, snuff dipper was a character that Will would never forget, and he brought plenty of laughs too.

When Mercer arrived at the base in July, Gunny Johnson remembered him from 29 Palms in California. Mercer had taught hand to hand combat in San Diego. The men slapped backs and shook hands, happy to see one another. The Gunny issued him a 45 and 782 gear.

Mercer asked, "What's goin' on Gunny?"

Gunny Johnson gave a positive report. "For now, we're livin' good. We have hard back tents and hot chow. There's a tank unit between us and Dog Patch that fires across the river every night. Other than that, enjoy it...while you can."

That night, Sergeant Mercer was drinking Vietnamese beer and got a little tipsy. The next day, July 4th 1965, very early in the morning, the Viet Cong attacked the base on the Air Force side and tragically killed most of the Air Force personnel. Then, a barefooted teenaged boy ran up the air strip and threw satchel charges under five C130 planes and blew them up.

As soon as the enemy mortars began exploding, the Marines ran to their positions. The Captain, the Gunny, Private Jones and Will Brown reported to Tower One and the EE8 phones began ringing.

Gunny Johnson picked up a phone and told the caller "We are manned and ready, Sir!"

The Captain shouted orders. "Brown, get another can of ammo for the machine gun and a dozen hand grenades!"

As mortars were exploding and tracers lighting up the night sky, Will saw Mercer running in his underwear and unlaced boots, biting on his sea bag. For a moment, he disappeared in one of the drain ditches, and then suddenly reappeared, rolling over and over while he was still biting on his sea bag.

Will stopped to make sure he was alright before he returned to the tower. When he was back, the Gunny asked Will what was happening with Mercer.

"He put the 45 you checked him out with in his sea bag and put a combination lock on it. It seems he forgot the combination."

The Viet Cong agressively attacked the Marines at Marble Mountain, but they were cut down with machine gun and rifle fire. When the sun came up, a surreal scene with dead men and disemboweled body parts lay below the two pillars of rock. And the kid who washed their clothing and polished their boots, nicknamed VC, was found dead, alongside the Viet Cong.

One afternoon, a weary Marine shuffled into the fort and asked, "Is there a Will Brown in this unit?"

Someone yelled, "Over in Tower One."

Will didn't recognize Pete Springer right away. With a second look, he ran to him and the two men hugged each other.

Will put his fist under Pete's chin and pushed it up to get a good look at his haggard face. "I can't tell you how glad I am to see you...and you're okay. Where's your unit?"

"I'm in the hills about three miles from here. We're dug in for a couple of days and the CO said I could come check on you. I lost my squad three days ago and they gave me a battlefield promotion to Corporal. Can you believe it? Will, I'm not the same person I used to be. I'm a hundred years older...and wiser too."

"That's great you got promoted! I'm proud of you Pete. You've come a long way. It's a crazy war. Yeah, it tends to age a guy. Partly because we don't get much sleep. Every time they told us we were gonna get hit, we stayed up all night and nothing happened. As soon as we relax, they hit us."

Pete nodded. "I know what you mean. Hear anything from home? How's Laverne doin'?"

"The doc told Laverne she's doing great and expects a healthy baby in a few months. Have you heard from Latoya?"

"Yep. She sends me chocolate chip cookies...here, you want one?" Pete pulled a couple broken cookies out of his pocket and Will took one. "And I want you to be the first to know...I've asked her to marry me."

"That's good news, Pete."

"Will, I want you to be my Best Man."

"I accept."

In the distance, the men were interupted with what sounded like rapid machine gun fire.

Pete stared at the sky and murmured, "I gotta get back. I'm gettin' twelve new men. I've been worried about taking a new leadership role, but my gunny said, 'If you treat them like they're your kids, they'll die for you.' But I don't want 'em to die Will."

Will could not hold back the tears as he looked at his war-worn friend and they hugged one another. "Semper Fi, Marine."

When Will returned to the fort, he found Gunny Johnson in dismay, bent over and pressing his forehead on his desk .

"What's wrong Gunny?"

"Brown, can you tell me how in the hell did Private Chorley get in the Corps? I have never seen such a screw up!"

"I guess he probably made some recruiter's quota for the month. What did he do now?"

Johnson pounded his desk with his fist. "I told him to burn out the Head. So he poured five gallons of gas on it and burned it to the ground. The Head was the only peaceful place I found in this God forsaken place."

Will saw that Johnson was tripping on the edge of sanity. The gunny bawled. "Its been one thing after another with that idiot. I had a box to keep my record books in. All I needed was a couple hinges on one side. I didn't think Chorley could foul up such a simple job. Right? Wrong. He brought it back with a hinge on both sides, battened down to where now, I can't get into it."

Will laughed but the depressed gunny was despondent and continued. "There's more. The Military Police just brought him into my office a little while ago and he's in trouble for emptying the soda machine outside of head-quarters. It's the one you put a coin in and slide the drink down the rail and pull it out. Well, Chorley was found with a bottle opener and a straw and had sucked all the bottles dry."

"You know, Brown, I tried to trade Chorley to the Air Force for half a beef. But they turned me down!"

29

Thorn Hill

Over the weeks, Will became close friends with Emile Anderson, an African American from Atlanta, Georgia. The two men shared personal information about their home life and general values, and soon found that they had a lot in common.

Will was on his way to Tower One with some supplies when Emile called to him.

"Hey Will! What's happening? Ain't the Captain back from that pow wow yet?"

"Yeah, He's back. I just saw him. He said he's going to call a meeting in the Mess Hall but he wouldn't tell me anything else."

"Oh – oh."

"Yeah, I know. Something's up."

The company assembled in the Mess Hall a few hours later and Captain Soehner made the fateful announcement.

"In three days, we'll be leaving the fort. In three days we'll move personnel and equipment by helicopters, five miles across the Danang River. We will be in enemy territory on a hill site we've named Thorn Hill."

"We have been advised there's movement on the Ho Chi Minh Trail by regular North Vietnamese units, heading south. The Force Recon platoon will provide initial security and daily intelligence as they watch for all movement."

"A small bulldozer will be air lifted in and Gunny Johnson and H & S personnel will construct the Command bunker in the center of the site. Sergeant Beltran and the First Platoon will set up bunkers on the left flank. Sergeant Rodriguez and the Second Platoon will set up bunkers on the right flank."

"Six listening post and designated Claymore mines and concertina are shown on your maps. We will be supported by close air support out of Danang with one company of 155 Howitzer's and offshore naval gunfire on standby if needed. Logistical support and Medevac will be by helicopter out of Danang. Four medical personnel have been assigned including one surgeon, one nurse and two corpsman."

Despite the negative impact of his words, Captain Soehner had the leadership ability to give the company confidence with his positive outlook. After his announcement was completed and he'd carefully elaborated on the details that the Marines needed to know, he added one more thing with gusto.

"Men, as I mentioned, we're calling the hill site, Thorn Hill. We have named it that because it will surely be a thorn in the side of the Viet Cong!"

The landing at Thorn Hill was a frenzy of well-planned coordination, and within one hour, the hill was secured with no casualties. The careful preparations in the move caught the Viet Cong by surprise.

Will and Emile Anderson shared a bunker, and on the first night, movement was noted, flares went up and the first mortars fell on the Hill. Coordinates were called in and the first napalm was dropped.

What seemed like seconds after the warnings, an NVA came within ten feet of their bunker. Will fired out of instinct and he killed his first human being. Then everything was frantic with the unforgettable, loathsome sounds of war for about a half hour.

When things settled down and became quiet, the soldiers lay on the moist ground with their rifles pointing into the darkness, listening and waiting for alerts or intruders, throughout the longest night of their lives. Many finding their own heartbeats deafening.

The next morning, Will was disturbed to see the VC soldier he had killed, gruesomely sprawled on the ground with his eyes still open.

The hideous sight of death and injury became commonplace at Thorn Hill and the surrounding areas of Vietnam, although no one could ever truly become desensitized to it. Most soldiers carried the abhorrent scenes of war all their lives, unable to erase them from their minds.

Life on the battlefield was surreal to many young men, some of whom had never left home until they enlisted or were drafted. But their unconceivable bravery was displayed every day, and the courageous Marines took chances to save the lives of many. Still, bravery didn't mean that there wasn't fear. Bravery met doing what was necessary despite their terror.

As the weeks progressed and causalities were counted, many soldiers felt impressed with the somber task of writing their last words for their families in case of their demise. Death was prevalent all around them.

Will and his friend, Emile had a heartfelt talk about what they could do for each other in case one of them was killed. They agreed to visit each other's family to help bring them comfort and closure. Both men had written letters which they wanted delivered to their loved ones in the event of their passing, and they gave each other the letter they wrote for safe keeping.

Will admitted his fears to Emile. "I don't want to end up in one of those body bags. I don't want to die before I see my unborn child. Aren't you afraid of dying, Emile?"

"Will, I don't want to die either. Anybody who says they aint scared is a liar. But I became a Christian and received Jesus Christ when I was twelve, and so if God should decide to take me, I'm ready. Ya gotta be ready Will. Nobody knows what tomorrow is gonna bring, and this life is a mere speck in eternity. I knows it. There's better livin' after this life."

Will explained, "I believe in God, and I guess it isn't that I'm really afraid of dying, but I just have to get back to Laverne. And our child will need a father. It's more about what they'll need."

Emile moved nearer Will. He laid his right hand on Will's helmet and began to pray in his husky voice. "My dear God, in the Name of Jesus, I pray for your divine blessin' upon my brother. Surround him with your Angels, keep him safe and give him your supernatural peace and strength..."

Emile hadn't finished praying when word was passed that movement was seen.

Sergeant Beltran was ordered to take two squads and set up an ambush at the sight where the enemy might be approaching.

As soon as it was dark, the First and Second Squads moved slowly and silently as possible through the brush towards the area where movement was seen. Claymores and grenade trip wires were inconspicuously set in place. Watches were set and they began waiting, trying not to breathe too loudly and hoping their noisy heartbeats would not alert the enemy.

At two that morning, Will Brown observed movement. At just the right time he set off the claymores and all hell broke loose. The movement sited was not just a squad as was thought earlier, but a platoon of NVA regulars.

It became a surreal and unspeakable battle scene with men being blown apart and others falling down wounded. Sergeant Beltran, two Corporals and three Privates were killed instantly. Corporal Reeves immediately called in for Medivacs.

Will remembered seeing the repugnant insides of a pig on the farm, but he'd never seen the insides of a human being like this. He watched the Corpsman pick up Sergeant Beltrans intestines from the dirt and place them back in his stomach. But there was no time for anyone to be sick or to grieve or to cry or to do anything but defend themselves from the ferocious, blood-thirsty enemy.

Firing continued as the dead and wounded were loaded on a chopper that landed. Eventually, Corporal Reeves loudly ordered the patrol to withdraw to Thorn Ridge. Will quickly began moving out and saw Corporal Shipman, who was only a few yards from him receive a heart wound and die two seconds later after he gasped pathetically, "Jesus, help."

When they returned to the ridge, a supply chopper received a direct mortar round and exploded inside the fire base. Gunny Johnson was calling in coordinates and after the first round fell, he yelled repeatedly, "Fire for effect. Fire for effect."

The NVA were ruthless and they kept regrouping the following days. The Marines would also regroup, wash out their helmets, replace ammo, make head calls and most prayed. If they were lucky, that might even be able to sleep a few minutes.

There was a sickening stench of burning flesh from the Napalm and the smell of rotting human bodies that the Marines would have in their nostrils forever.

Early on the third of August, Will and Emile shared a piece of beef jerky in their bunker and were conversing about the war.

Will asked Emile, "Have you noticed the difference between the Mustang officers that came up through the ranks verses the ones that came out of the Academy?"

Emile said, "The Mustang officers seem to have more dependence on their NCO'S."

Will agreed, "Yeah, I think they do. But honestly, Emile, sometimes it feels like the blind is leading the blind over here."

Emile responded, "Will, we're all pretty much blind...really. In fact, the Bible says 'For now we see through a glass, darkly; but then face to face: now

I know in part; but then shall I know even as also I am known.' I don't mind telling you my friend, I look forward to seeing it all clearly."

Later that same day, a North Vietnamese battalion attacked the ridge. A barrage of mortars fell on the ridge, and with an unrelenting suicidal force, the enemy infiltrated the perimeter. Three NVA soldiers came within a few feet of Will and Emile's bunker. Will shot two of them, but while he was inserting another clip, the third soldier pointed his rifle at Will and was ready to shoot.

Emile dived in front of Will and fired at the soldier, shooting him dead the same second that their enemy pulled the trigger. Emile received the round that was meant for Will in his stomach.

Will tried to stop Emile's bleeding but it was a fatal wound. As Will looked at Emile, a strange glow came over his face and he appeared to be looking far off, but then he looked back at Will and smiled and whispered, "Will, I see the light."

Emile died in Will's arms as Will rocked him back and forth. And Will moaned despairingly.

Will's grief caused him to function on automatic in the next days. As always, there really was no time to grieve or cry or do anything but keep on keeping on. And he did everything numbly.

Four days after Emile's death, Captain Soehner came to Will's bunker with a card in his hand. "Will, I was going through Emile's personal effects to send to his family and I found this. I believe he would want you to have it."

Will took the card from Soehner and the Captain left him alone to read it. It was in Emile's handwriting and it said, "GREATER LOVE HATH NO MAN THAN THIS, THAT A MAN LAY DOWN HIS LIFE FOR HIS FRIENDS."

The NVA suffered great losses in their continued attempts to overrun the ridge. Yet their tenacity to take the ridge was almost as strong as the Marine's to defend it.

Private Rankin was hit as he withdrew from his listening post thirty yards from the perimeter. Will saw it happen and heroically crawled to Rankin in order to drag him to safety. As he moved him across the ground, Will was hit twice in his right leg. Will felt a burning sensation and looked down to see blood pouring out of his leg.

122

Both Rankin and Will were taken to the Dannag hospital by a Medivac chopper. And early in the morning, Will woke up to find himself in a hospital bed with a nurse adjusting his IV and a doctor standing over him. He was told it had been necessary to amputate his right leg at the knee.

30

Hospitalization

It was a sunny day in Beckley, West Virginia. Laverne was showing her mother the soft, pink and blue blanket that her mother-in-law, Velma Brown, had knitted for the baby-to-be. She happened to look out the window and saw a Captain and a sergeant in a Marine uniform get out of their vehicle and walk to the front door.

Fearing the worst, Laverne immediately turned pale. Seeing her daughter's face, Nina Alderman asked Laverne what was wrong, thinking that perhaps she was having early labor pains, but Laverne rushed to the front door witihout answering.

Laverne opened the front door to the two men before they had a chance to knock, she looked at their grim faces and began to cry when the Captain spoke.

"Are you Mrs. Will Brown?"

Unable to speak, Laverne nodded her head. Her mother approached the door and stood beside her as the Captain continued.

"Mrs. Brown, I'm here to inform you that your husband was wounded in action and he is in the hospital in Okinanwa, Japan."

Laverne faltered and her mother grabbed her and put her arm around her for support.

Laverne stammered, "He's not dead?"

"No ma'am. He was wounded, and I'm so sorry to say that this is all the information we have at this time."

The sergeant handed Laverne some paperwork with the address and whereabouts of the hospital, the date he was admitted, a few other details and then the men left. Laverne and her mother moved shakily to the couch, sat down, and held each other and cried.

Laverne was on her way out the door to share the report with Will's parents when the phone rang. A nurse from the hospital in Okinawa asked to speak to Laverne Brown, so Nina called her back inside to get the phone.

Laverne's heart was beating very fast when she said, "Hello. This is Laverne Brown."

It was Will's voice at the other end.

"Honey, I'm okay."

"Oh...Will!...Will! What happened? Are you really okay?" The tears ran from Lavernes eyes and fell on her blue cotton maternity blouse, soaking her round belly."

"I'll be alright, Laverne. But a bad thing happened. I need to prepare you. I got hit twice in my right leg..." Will forced himself to say it without feelings, although the emotional agony was welling up inside of him like a bomb that would soon burst. "Laverne, they had to amputate."

Laverne gasped, "Oh God!"

Will bravely continued speaking before he lost it. "I can't talk to you any more right now, but in two weeks they're flying me to the rehab in Charleston. I'll see you soon my darling. I love you."

Will gave the phone to the nurse and she kindly hung up the receiver and left him in privacy.

Nina Alderman drove Laverne to the Brown farm. She wanted to support her in relating the hard news to Will's parents. It was devastating for them to hear that Will had lost a leg, but after they had wept together for a long while, they rejoiced that he was alive and prayed together for Will's healing.

Fourteen days later, Laverne, Walter and Velma drove to Charleston and arrived at Jimmy T's home where they planned to stay for a few days. Jimmy T had continued to do very well with his dry cleaning business and he owned a new home that had plenty of room for guests. Walter was particularly impressed with the plumbing.

The military had provided Laverne with the estimated time of arrival of Will's flight so they all waited at the air strip when the plane landed and taxied up to the terminal.

Will was the third person to appear exiting the plane with the help of a medical assistant. They were astounded to see he was upright, and although unsteadily, he was walking with a cane. His family didn't know that he had already received his artificial leg from Hawaii.

With tears of joy, they embraced him. Then the assistant helped him to get in a wheelchair and he was taken in a special vehicle to the Charleston rehabilitation hospital.

Will's parents visited him at the hospital each day while they were in Charleston. Laverne stayed at his bedside and during his rehab exercises as often as she could. The first night she even spent the night on a cot beside his hospital bed that the staff had kindly provided for her.

On the third day, a Lieutenant and a First Sergeant came into the room while Laverne was standing beside Will's bed. They saluted Will as they entered and Will sat up and saluted them. The Lieutenant spoke first.

"Sometimes it takes a while for things to go through the chain of command. You may want to know that Captain Soehner requested that you be honored for saving the life of Private Rankin by making you a recipient of the Silver Star." The Lieutenant walked near the bed.

"May I?" The Lieutenant then pinned the Silver Star medal and the Purple Heart on Will's hospital pajamas and both men saluted Will again. "Congratulations, Sir."

The sergeant said, "Thank you for your service to our country."

As they left, Will saw his mom and dad standing in the doorway glowing with pride because they'd heard everything that was said.

Meanwhile, a surprised Laverne had put her hands around her belly after her water broke. "Dear Lord, I don't know if this country girl can take this celebrity status of her husband being a hero."

Not realizing that Laverne was going into labor, Will teasingly mimicked, "Dear Lord, I don't know if this country boy can take this celebrity status of being a hero."

What was happening to Laverne was obvious to Velma. She immediately went over to Laverne and took her arm to lead her out of the room, and smiling at Will said, "Apparently this country baby wants to be a part of the celebrity status with daddy and mommy!"

A beautiful, bouncing baby girl weighing six pounds, twelve ounces and twenty inches long, was born three weeks earlier than anticipated, and the arrival of Mercedes Ann Brown brought joy to the entire family.

After a short stay in Charleston, Walter and Velma needed to get back to the farm. But Laverne and Mercedes stayed at Jimmy T's house until Will was released from rehab.

One day before his release, Will had three visitors. Private Rankin's mother, father and twelve year old sister knocked on the door of his room and entered solemnly. Mr. Rankin shook hands with him and introduced his family. Then Mrs. Rankin spoke.

"Will Brown, we came here to Charleston from our home in New Jersey in order to express our gratitude to you. Our son told us what happened. We want to thank you for saving his life."

Weeping, the mother hugged Will, followed by the sister and the suddenly speechless father. Will felt their deep appreciation, but he also felt their too obvious sympathy for what he had endured in the loss of his leg. He changed their uncomfortable focus by asking about Private Rankin's condition, and he was told that Rankin had lost a kidney but was doing better. Like so many families who had sons injured in the war, Will could see the suffering on the faces of this family.

It was not merely the soldiers who suffered. The families ached during the many days of not knowing if there son or daughter was safe, of desperately missing them, of hearing frightening reports in the newspapers and on newsreels, of waiting for letters, of receiving the letters with hideous descriptions and homesickness, of worry and unanswered questions. They agonized as they listened to the President and military leaders speak about the necessity of this continuing war, but they also heard the disdainful and rebellious individuals who mocked those who joined the effort. They watched the loud-mouthed picketers and protestors and those who really knew nothing of the sacrifices made for freedom. And sometimes they couldn't help but question whether the supposedly peace-loving people who denied the need for involvement of their sons and daughters on the other side of the world, could be right, after all.

31

Promises Kept

Will had worked very hard to get his strength back while he was at the Charleston Rehabilitation Hospital, and the personnel at the hospital knew he was an exceptional patient. Many soldiers lost the will to live and weren't motivated to pursue rehabilitation. Their battle scars went much deeper than lost arms or legs. But Will's positive attitude helped him to push himself. And at last, he could walk again, no longer needing a wheelchair or a cane.

Will told Laverne they would go to Atlanta to see Emile's family as soon as they were able to make the trip. When Mercedes was almost eight months old, he and his wife and child flew to Atlanta Georgia.

Upon arriving, they checked into a hotel, unpacked, and enjoyed a supper of ham and cheese sandwiches which Laverne had prepared and packed before they left. In the morning after Mercedes had been bathed and fed, they took a taxi to the apartment complex which was once Emile's home.

The apartment was in an impoverished area of the city. They walked down the dark, windowless hallway of the building that had colorful graffiti on the dirty walls. Among the words and abstract artwork sketched on the sheetrocked walls were symbols signifying gangs, phone numbers for "A good time," a remarkably realistic drawing of a horse and an eagle, and words severely scrawled in black that said, "Where is God?"

After finding the correct apartment number, Will knocked on the door.

Emile's sixteen year old brother answered the door and was surprised to see a young white family standing in the hallway.

Will was taken aback at the similarity in appearance the boy had to Emile, but he recovered himself and asked for Mrs. Anderson.

A cheerful-looking, heavy set woman, wearing an apron which had seen better days, came to the door. "Can I help you?"

Will began slowly. "Mrs. Anderson, my name is Will Brown. Your son, Emile, was my friend."

"Oh...my...Lord." The woman pressed her fingers to her cheeks. "You Will? My son wrote about you. You was his best friend. Please come on in."

128

She looked at Laverne and the baby asleep in her arms.

After Will introduced Laverne and Mercedes, they all sat down in the small living area while Mrs. Anderson made over Mercedes. "Emile wrote me that y'all were expectin'. My, my, ain't she sweet! God bless you for visitin' us."

Eventually, Will had the opportunity to share what had happened in the last moments of Emile's life and how her son died in his arms.

Mrs. Anderson asked, "Did my baby have any last words?"

"Yes. A strange glow came over his face...and he appeared to be looking far off somewhere. Then he looked back at me and smiled and said, 'Will, I see the light.'"

Mrs. Anderson raised her arms over her head while tears flowed from her round face. "Praise God. He seen Jesus!" Then she nodded her head silently while tears continued to fall. "I knew my boy was saved, but I never knowed he'd be going to see the Lord...before his mama."

Will gave her the card with the Bible verse that the Commanding officer had found in her son's personal belongings. Then he told her and Emile's brother that Emile was a hero and how grateful he was that he had saved his life.

When the Browns rose to leave the apartment, Mrs. Anderson said, "I can't tell you what this visit has meant to me." Then she kissed and hugged each one of them. Mercedes, who was asleep during their visit, finally awoke, focused her little eyes on the lady's dark, shiny face, and gave her an endearing baby smile.

Before they walked out the door, Will pulled the letter out of his pocket which Emile had written for his family in case of his death. He had purposely waited to give it to Mrs. Anderson so she could read it in private. He placed it in her thick hands, and when she saw the handwriting, she tenderly clenched the letter to her breast and nodded her thanks repeatedly.

In the taxi on the way back to the Hotel, Will told Laverne, "It was a shock to see Emile's brother. He looked so much like Emile. And although Emile had told me his family was poor, I didn't expect to see a place like that."

Laverne looked at Will knowingly, realizing that the evening had brought difficult memories. "Will, I was impressed with Emile's mother and his brother. And even though they are poor as this world knows poverty, I can see they are truly rich in God's love."

32

To Kill and to Destroy

Sunday morning at the Beckley Assembly of God Church, Velma Brown was feeling especially thankful that all her family was in church. Little Becky had fallen asleep on Walter's shoulder. Milford, Will, Laverne and Nina Alderman were sitting in the pew in front of them, and Mercedes was in the nursery.

Pastor Dan was concluding his sermon. "...So as I close my message, I hope you will remember that verse in John 10:10 that I've spoken on. I'll read it one more time. 'The thief does not come except to steal, and to kill, and to destroy. I have come that they may have life, and that they may have it more abundantly.' True life only comes through Jesus Christ. I pray that each of you find it. Amen."

After the hymn, "Have Thine Own Way" was sung, the congregation began moving out of the sanctuary. Will and Laverne were moving towards the nursery to pick up Mercedes when they spotted Frankie Ragsdale, dressed in Marine greens, standing near the back pew. Frankie began walking towards Will. Laverne, glanced at Frankie, and seeing his unusual peaceful expression, nodded, and went on to the nursery, leaving the men alone together.

Frankie greeted Will and stuck out his hand, so Will shook hands with him. "Will, I've got orders for Nam...and Pastor Dan encouraged me to make things right with everyone before I leave. I feel obligated to apologize for being such a damn asshole." He looked around to see if any church member had heard the words that slipped out. A short, dimpled, grey-haired lady who was walking by, overheard and chuckled softly. Frankie turned to her briefly, "Sorry."

The elderly woman, aware of Frankie's previous, notorious reputation, responded, "That's alright. God bless you son. Confession is good for the soul...and it's about time!" and continued walking.

"Yes, Ma'am.

Frankie faced Will and continued with what he needed to say. "The Marines gave me the training and the discipline I never got from my dad, and I'm seeing things differently." Frankie's eyes searched Will's face, not knowing how he would respond.

Finally, Will responded by putting his arms around his half brother and hugging him. "My ass kickin' days are over, Frankie."

Back at the Brown farm, Velma had a large pork roast cooking in the oven while they were all at church. The kitchen smelled heavenly when they returned home. Little Becky was setting the table, and Walter was holding Mercedes in his lap and enjoying her full attention when the telephone rang.

Laverne answered the phone and heard Pete Springer's girlfriend, Latoya, sobbing on the other end. Latoya's words were hard to understand because of her wailing. Eventually it became dreadfully clear that Pete's mother told Latoya that two Marine's came to the Springer household and informed them that Pete had been killed by a grenade in Vietnam.

The phone fell from Laverne's hand and she wept. Everyone in the room became silent and Will asked, "Honey, what's wrong?"

Will's heart was broken when he realized he would never see his best friend again, and he grieved many days.

Will was one of the coffin bearers at Pete's military funeral. The coffin bearers, the firing squad, the Senior Sergeant and the officer in charge were all dressed in blue.

As the taps were blown, vivid memories of Pete raced through Will's mind. Among them, Will remembered when Pete first advised him about dating Laverne, the sardines he always ate, finding him at the recruiter's office, the trip to Parris Island, cutting off the sleeves of his uniform to keep cool, the trouble he got into, the brig with the bulldog, Laverne's missing peanut butter cookies, and the last moments with him.

Unashamed and remaining dignified, the tears rolled down Will's face as he thought of his friend—and so many others who had died, who had suffered, and whose lives were changed forever in Vietnam.

The coffin bearers ceremoniously folded the flag and gave it to the senior NCO, and there wasn't a dry eye in the place when he presented it to Pete's mother. "On behalf of the President of the United States, and a grateful nation."

Since Will had received an honorary discharge, Will, Laverne and

Mercedes, moved into the Brown farmhouse. Walter Brown finally had allowed Jimmy T to help with the renovation and modernization of the house although he refused to give up the old outhouse. Even though the home was comfortable enough, Will and Laverne dreamed of a day when they could have a home built on the 180 acres that Will's real father, Hollis Ragsdale had bequeathed to Will.

Meanwhile, Will continued to hear devastating reports of men killed and injured in Vietnam, some of the men were those with whom he had served. The war was by no means over, and The U.S. involvement in Vietnam fighting continued into the early seventies.

In 1969, when Mercedes was almost four years old, an ammunitions truck was blown up in Vietnam, and Frankie Ragsdale was killed, just months after he'd re-enlisted.

33

Life More Abundantly

Will Brown inherited the entire Ragsdale estate. The great Ragsdale house that had impressed him with such magnificence was now his own. And after all the property deeds were transferred and ownership papers were given to him by the aging lawyer, Jim Davis, Will drove Laverne and Mercedes to the house so they could see what now belonged to them.

As they drove towards the enormous, plantation style home, they wondered who had been taking such good care of the grounds. The lawns were nicely cut and the landscaping was in excellent condition. Everything looked too pristine for a place that had supposedly been vacated months ago.

Eyes wide and excited about her new home, Mercedes asked, "Daddy, is there a swing set in the back yard?"

Will laughed. "I don't know if there is, but I know there is a swimming pool."

Before they got to the massive front door, Ragsdale's elderly servant with the strange chortling voice opened the door. He was the one who held his chin so high that Will once wondered how he could see beyond his nose.

He stood in front of them blurting tensely, "Good morning, Master Brown, Mrs. Brown and Miss Brown. I'm indeed happy to see you. If you should need my services, I will stay and work for you. If not, I shall immediately go to the servants quarters and pack my things and remove myself from these premises. I have been in charge of the grounds, the house, the maid service, the cook, the vehicles and all the employees of this household for thirty-five years; nevertheless, I shall go if that is what you desire. Please advise me."

The couple wasn't prepared for the abrupt greeting and didn't know what to say. Laverne noticed the gentleman's eyes were tearing up in anticipation of their response, so she spoke. "What is your name, Sir?"

"My name is Grayson Beckett Fin, madam. Mr. Hollis called me Fin. You may call me Fin, if you like." The well-mannered gentleman peered over his nose at the pretty young woman who stood before him while he dabbed his eyes with a silk handkerchief.

"Fin, by the looks of things, I think we will need you."

Will smiled and nodded his agreement, approvingly.

Mercedes had been studying the stern, but emotional servant. Then she broke the momentary silence and piped, "I'm Mercedes. Is there is a swing set in the back yard?"

Surprisingly, the sophisticated man knelt down to Mercedes' level and with his chin still held high declared, "There is indeed a rather marvelous tire swing which belonged to the late Frankie, Ragsdale that perhaps you would be interested in."

Mercedes squealed with glee and grabbed his hand. Charming him with her bright, dimpled smile, she earnestly said, "Let's go see it!"

Epilogue

Over the years, Will and Laverne shared their wealth with their family. They also gave generous contributions to the church and the Disabled Veterans organization. Along with the help of Fin, who adored their daughter, they brought up Mercedes well, teaching her right priorities. Even though they'd become millionaires, they remained the happy, friendly, country boy and girl that the Beckley, West Virginia community had always known.

Will and Laverne often hosted church and community related gatherings on the beautiful grounds of their estate. One afternoon at a picnic in their yard, Pastor Dan asked Will to entertain the group by speaking about his experience in the Marine Corp.

After he had spoken about his experiences for a while, Will concluded with the following words:

> "I was in the forefront of battle in Vietnam, but there is another kind of battle that every human encounters. I've learned the most important fight is spiritual—and God has given each of us an assignment in this combat. He's looking for men and women who will stay on their knees. And if we will choose to enlist in this great battle, someday we'll shout in Heaven, 'Not one was lost!'"

Will's brother, Milford, enlisted in the Marines as soon as he was old enough, and he enjoyed many years with a military career.

When she was eighteen, Little Becky surprised everyone when she became engaged to Vernon Pitts. He was the boy she "hated" as a child because he received more points at show 'n tell for his uncle's medal of honor.

Jimmy T. retired from his successful dry cleaning business before he got too old to enjoy the profits.

Walter and Velma Brown happily remained in the beloved farm house which was updated again, although Walter insisted on keeping the outhouse for sentimental reasons.

Nina Alderman enjoyed traveling and was often found on a cruise ship.

Radar became very protective of Mercedes. (But much to Fin's dismay, he's still crapping on the floor, rubbing his nose in it and jumping out the window.)

Photographs That Helped Shape this Book
from Herbert H. Roebuck's Collection

Color Guard at Citizenship ceremony in Fresno, California, August 1968.
(Herbert Roebuck is second from the left holding American flag.)

Two U.S. Marines from Platoon 101 are practicing their shooting on the firing range at Parris Island.

This former French Compound outside of Danang was abandoned after the French-Vietnam War and was used by U.S. Military forces during the sixties.

This is a water well that was in the middle of Danang.
It was a main water resource frequented by the local people in 1965.

During the war in Vietnam, an infamous village just outside Danang was named
"Dogpatch" by the U.S. Marines. It was a patch of land which was home
for impoverished people who lived in small huts and there were lots of feral dogs.

The Hawk Missile Site was located on top of Hill 327 overlooking the Danang River. The missile was pointed precisely to what was once a Viet Cong controlled area.

On July 4, 1965, a skinny, barefoot, Viet Cong teenager ran up the center of the runway and threw satchel charges under each of these planes.

Herb's 1970 Retirement Ceremony: From left to right is Major Justice, Sergeant Roebuck, Herb's wife, Willie Mae, and daughters Pam (age 11) and Lynn (age 7).

In 2011, many years after the Vietnam War, a sign and a hat
was placed on this skeleton at the Rehabilitation Center in Clovis, California
to remind everyone that once a Marine—always a Marine...even after retirement.
("Semper Fidelis," i.e. always faithful, is the U.S. Marine Corps motto.)

140

www.ingramcontent.com/pod-product-compliance
Lightning Source LLC
Chambersburg PA
CBHW020407030726
47496CB00007B/2353